ERRAND OF LOVE

Jancy Talliman flies halfway around the world to Bungalan, in Australia, to renew an interrupted love affair with Michael Rickwood, who she'd met in London. She remains undaunted on discovering that he's unofficially engaged to Cynthia Meddow, especially given the support of Michael's brother Quentin, and his sister Susan. Jancy settles in a small town nearby. Then as she becomes involved with the towns-people, dam worker Arnulf, and Quentin, Jancy alters the very reason for her long journey south . . .

A. C. WATKINS

ERRAND OF LOVE

Complete and Unabridged

LINFORD
Leicester

First published in Great Britain in 1974 by
Robert Hale & Company
London

First Linford Edition
published 2008
by arrangement with
Robert Hale Limited
London

Copyright © 1974 by A. C. Watkins

British Library CIP Data

Watkins, A. C.
  Errand of love.—Large print ed.—
Linford romance library
1. English—Australia—Fiction
2. Love stories 3. Large type books
I. Title
823.9'14 [F]

ISBN 978–1–84782–489–9

Published by
F. A. Thorpe (Publishing)
Anstey, Leicestershire

Set by Words & Graphics Ltd.
Anstey, Leicestershire
Printed and bound in Great Britain by
T. J. International Ltd., Padstow, Cornwall

This book is printed on acid-free paper

To my daughter Susan

1

As the twin-carriage diesel train came to a halt, Jancy Talliman picked up her suitcase and looked out of the window.

She hadn't expected a rainbow at journey's end. Not exactly. But the long, hot and tedious trip from Sydney, over steep ranges and across dusty plains, had soon dulled the lustre of her expectations.

This shabby, weather-worn railway platform, with its neglected air, paint-flaked ticket office and destination board reading 'Bungalan', seemed the end of the world.

Another world, far removed from swinging London. Another country, twelve thousand miles from home. The far country; the rough and rugged land she'd read about and heard about and, being an island unto herself, couldn't have cared less about.

With a fleeting dismay Jancy gazed through the smeared glass, wishing again that she had written to Michael of her arrival in Australia. But she had intended the meeting to be a surprise, a wonderful reunion, a joy and happiness she had tended and nurtured since leaving England ten days before.

England, she thought, homesick already for familiar places and faces.

From Kensington to Bungalan. From the throbbing heart and bloodstreams of a gay and wide-awake metropolis to a dreary country village in New South Wales.

Her friends had given her ample warning. At a farewell party in the backroom workshop of the Teen and Twenties boutique, again at a moist-eyed pre-departure dinner, when tears had flowed copiously, and, finally, in the airport lounge.

'You're sure this is what you want, Jancy? You're absolutely positive? You're not taking off on a fool's errand?'

An errand it was, to be sure, though

not a fool's errand. An errand of love. Too long she had permitted her head to rule her heart. Too long she had unselfishly relegated herself to second place.

When Aunt Edith Talliman died and Jancy inherited her sole relative's worldly goods and wealth, she became free at last. The cage door was open and, after years of comforting and caring for the frail old woman, she could fly wherever she chose.

There was only one place to which she wanted to fly. Australia. And to have tall, dark and captivating Michael Rickwood hold her in his arms again.

Jancy opened the carriage door and stepped out. The summer heat was blinding. One heel caught in the rough boards and, off-balance, she stumbled.

'Steady, there,' called the station attendant, a lean and gangling teenager in shirt sleeves and braces. 'The platform's a bit tricky. Regulars watch their step.'

'I shouldn't think you'd have too

3

many of those,' Jancy told him, squinting in the glare and wishing she'd worn a wide-brimmed hat.

The youth laughed and took her ticket.

'You're the only passenger on this train. And a stranger to boot. Anyone special looking out for you?'

Jancy shook her head. 'No, but very soon I'll be looking out for a hotel. I'll be wanting overnight accommodation. Is there one in town?'

There was none in sight. Behind the platform was a pot-holed gravel street, a few cottages and a sandstone church fenced with towering pines. Farther back was a scattering of other dwellings, many of them huddled under the boughs of shading trees. Beyond those, grazing land spread to distant hills.

The youth swung round and pointed. 'Turn left at the church and you'll see the shops. The pub is called the Empire and it's a couple of hundred yards along on the other side of the road.'

He stared at Jancy with open

curiosity and appreciation. A bold, big-boy stare that travelled vertically from her shoulder-length, honey-coloured hair to her beige shoes. 'Staying long?'

'That depends,' Jancy answered evasively, amused rather than embarrassed by the teenage scrutiny.

There was no cab in sight, no other means of transport. Lifting her suitcase and almost overpowered by the shimmering blaze of sunlight, Jancy walked dispiritedly down the ramp in the direction of the Anglican church.

Past it, and turning the corner, her worst fears were confirmed. It really was the living end.

The Bungalan business centre spread higgledy-piggledy, on both sides of a wide main street. She noticed a grocery store, a garage, a bakery and the Empire hotel, the latter flanked on the western side by a two-storey terrace of narrow-fronted shops, including a haberdashery; on the other, by a fruit-and-vegetables stall and a newsagency. A number of premises were unoccupied and, judging by their appearance, had been that way for a considerable time.

The hotel was a weatherboard building, with a full-fronted balcony overlooking the street.

Jancy's heart gave an odd lurch. The dilapidated hotel seemed as ancient as the railway station, its iron roof rusted brown. A one-night stopover would be more than adequate in such dismal surroundings.

But she had no choice. That afternoon she hoped to meet Michael Rickwood again, face to face, to assure him of the constancy of her love and devotion.

Six months ago, in his Earl's Court flat, Michael had asked Jancy to marry him. But, with patience and affection, she had been caring for Aunt Edith and the ill and aged woman was a responsibility that could neither be shared nor denied. She had tried to explain this moral obligation, this duty and dependency she alone must shoulder, but Michael, impatient and possessive, had been unable

6

or unwilling to understand.

'Couldn't we wait a little while?' Jancy had pleaded. 'I'm all she has left, and she needs me. Where would she go, what would she do . . . ? Please, darling, six months . . . '

'I can't even wait six days,' he told her, his hurt pride and wounded vanity lashing her in anger. 'I've had a letter from my brother Quentin. Mother insists I return home to Irongates.

'I've been over here four months, not a bad break for someone previously considered indispensable. And off the leash longer than I'd ever thought possible. Listen, sweetheart, we could be married immediately and fly home together. A week's honeymoon in Sydney, then on to the homestead . . . '

She'd argued, she'd tried to reason with him, present her point of view, to compromise, but in the end, defeated by her loyalty, he had gone off alone.

A fortnight later, Aunt Edith had died quietly in her sleep.

Remembering, Jancy sighed and

transferred the suitcase to her other hand. Renewing regrets was a worthless pastime.

Aunt Edith Talliman, a wise old woman who had kept abreast of the times and had her own maxims for day-by-day problems and decisions, had the marvellous capacity for reducing mountains to molehills.

'If at first you don't succeed, make a pot of tea and try again.'

And when, years back, Jancy had been considering alternative offers of employment, the boutique or layout artist with a departmental store: 'If you take the plunge, don't come up and take stock. Start swimming immediately. Your special talent lies in design, in flair and originality. If I were ten years younger, I'd wear your style of clothes myself. I rather fancy this mod gear.'

Dear, kind, gentle and with-it Aunt Edith. Jancy's only relative, only tie. A semi-invalid, the old lady had never known of Michael Rickwood's proposal, had never suspected her comforting niece had nursed a broken heart.

A room was available at the Empire. As she signed the register the portly, florid-faced hotelkeeper by name of Samuel Fowler eyed her speculatively and called, in a strident, upstairs voice for Sigrid.

'Take Miss Talliman's bag,' he told the slim blonde girl when she came hurrying from the back of the premises to the lobby office. 'She's got the Blue Room.'

Preceding her up the stairs, the housemaid asked pertinently: 'Staying long?'

The station assistant had asked the same question.

'At least one night.'

'That's enough in this place,' the girl said chattily. 'I ought to know. I live here.'

'Sigrid . . . ' Jancy paused for a moment and pondered on the name. The stairs were steep. 'Scandinavia?'

'Norwegian,' the girl corrected. 'Sigrid Vigeland. We came out here ten years ago. My brother Arnulf works on the Warabee dam, twelve miles up the valley. My father, too. He's an engineer. Given half a chance, I'd join them.'

'Are women employed at the dam?'

'In the canteen. Hundreds of men are on the project, building the earthen wall. Anywhere would be better than this pub.' She pulled a face. 'Hotel maid, that's me. Oh, it's so deadly dull.'

As she started climbing again and amused by the girl's instant confessions and disarming prattle, Jancy went on: 'What would you rather be doing?'

'Sewing,' Sigrid said. 'I just adore sewing. That's a nice dress you're wearing, Miss Talliman. Where did you buy it?'

The maid stopped for a second time and pointed to Jancy's sleeveless pink shift.

'I didn't buy it,' Jancy said. 'I designed it myself and had it made, in the shop where I used to work.'

'You couldn't get anything as groovy as that in this place,' Sigrid told her.

'The dress is fab, really it is. I wish someone would design me an original.'

Jancy smiled, warming to the girl and her effervescent nature. They reached the head of the stairs, walked along a hall and Sigrid ushered her through the last doorway on the left.

'This is the Blue Room,' she announced grandly. Then, in a conspirator's whisper: 'Ever seen anything as awful?'

The Blue Room had blue walls, blue patterned linoleum, and floral curtains in blue and yellow. There was a double bed, concave in the middle and covered with a blue chenille spread; a chest of drawers, a single wardrobe and, incredibly, a white-painted hatstand of Victorian vintage.

Noticing the stunned expression on Jancy's face, Sigrid smothered a giggle. 'Well, it's plain to be seen that you haven't. Still, you're lucky. The Green Room across the hall is a scream. And the Pink Room . . . '

Jancy laughed ruefully. 'I expect this

one will serve the purpose.'

'The bathroom's at the top of the stairs,' the maid went on. She opened a pair of stained glass french doors and stepped out on to the balcony.

'It's much cooler out here. Not that there's anything special to look at, except the passing traffic. And there's a terrific lot of that, since they detoured the valley road through here. It's part of the coastal highway, you see. Thirty miles that way,' she pointed east, 'to Canberra . . . ' — Canberra was the national capital and the fastest-growing city in Australia — ' . . . and seventy miles that way,' Sigrid pointed east, 'to the coast and seaside holiday resorts.'

She gazed at Jancy for a moment, then went on with disarming candour: 'You're English?'

Jancy nodded.

'I thought so. The refined accent. At the dam you get a mixture of everything — German, Polish, Italian, Irish, American . . . '

From below came Samuel Fowler's

reverberating summons. 'Sig-rid! Sig-rid!'

'There goes the old foghorn again.' The blonde girl sighed. 'He gets his money's worth, I can tell you. Sometimes I'd like to lock him in a sauna bath and throw away the key.'

As she started to leave, Jancy said quickly, 'I'm wanting to visit a property called Irongates. You've heard of it?'

'I should say so,' Sigrid said. 'Everyone knows Irongates, and the Rickwood family. It's about eight miles to the south. Three miles along the highway you make a right-hand turn at the signpost to Carsella. That's another village. Irongates is halfway.'

'How would I get there?' Jancy asked.

Sigrid pursed her lips, pondering.

'You can't walk, that's for sure. But occasionally Mr George — he manages the service station on the corner — rents out his own car to licensed drivers. Can you drive?'

'Yes.'

'Well then, you're practically there.

Want me to arrange it?'

'I'd be most grateful,' Jancy said. Clearly, the hotel maid was intelligent as well as pretty. 'For two o'clock?'

After a greasy, unpalatable lunch of fried chops and eggs in the hotel dining room, Jancy showered and changed.

Then she stood in front of the small, fly-specked mirror attached to the wardrobe and brushed her long, brown-gold hair until it gleamed. An emerald headband to complement the green dress, a pat of powder of the pale scattering of freckles and she was ready for the ordeal ahead.

It was one-fifty and she had ten minutes to wait. Here, alone in this pathetic hotel room, so close to Michael in distance and so removed in days and weeks and months, the enormity of the situation momentarily engulfed her.

Steady, she told herself firmly. For better or worse, you're one step removed from journey's end. Aunt Edith would have approved. Aunt Edith would have cheered you on.

14

But Aunt Edith was now a memory and the cheers and encouragements of yesterday were hushed for ever.

You're on your own now, Jancy said inwardly, trying to quell the butterflies of apprehension. You chose a course of action when you bought that air ticket. You weighed the matter thoroughly; the pros and the cons, the possibles and the improbables, the perhapses and the maybes.

Out of the past came an echo of Aunt Edith's soft and persuasive voice. 'You have the ability, the moral fibre, the resilience to do anything you want. Plunge and swim, there's a good girl. And have fun in the water.'

Half a dozen cars sped by. Suddenly feeling bleak and disconsolate, Jancy moved out on to the balcony.

For a few moments the golden afternoon was held in a vacuum. Then suddenly it was shattered by a shrill cacophony of birdtalk, a crazy chorus of chirpings and twitterings. It came from a colony of sparrows, perched on the wires strung between electric-light poles on the other side of the street. A hundred or more, they crowded side by side in long rows, flitting from wire to wire, jostling and pecking each other and trilling noisily.

'Oh, there you are,' came Sigrid's voice. 'Well, it's fixed and it isn't fixed. You're right for Irongates but not with Mr George. Quentin's taking you.'

Jancy swung round. 'Quentin Rick-wood?'

'I was at the garage when he drove in for petrol,' Sigrid explained. 'The car Mr George rents out was on the hoist — so I asked Quentin.'

'It's not a one-way trip to Irongates,' Jancy protested. 'I have to get back.'

'Not to worry,' the girl reassured her. 'Quentin's a real swinger. He'll do anything you want.'

'That's most hospitable. But he doesn't even know me.' And then Jancy thought, with foreboding: I'm not even sure he knows of me. What if I'm a stranger to the entire family?

Sigrid went on: 'You don't sell things, do you? Kitchen gadgets, encyclopaedias, insurance . . . Quentin was wondering.'

She could understand the curiosity directed at a newcomer in town, but was keeping her own counsel. Her purpose in Bungalan could become public property soon enough.

'No.' Jancy shook her head. 'I'll explain to Quentin as we go along.'

'You won't have much time for talking,' the hotel maid warned. 'He drives his Jaguar like a demon.'

'I've been in Jaguars before,' Jancy pointed out. 'I'll suggest he conform to the speed limits.'

Sigrid chuckled. 'You don't know Quentin. He doesn't conform to anything. He's a proper rebel.'

At first sight, she didn't doubt it. Quentin Rickwood and the E-type sports car made an incongruous pair. The high gloss and sleek lines of the bright red high-powered British import, with its spoke wheels, recessed headlamps and chromed accessories, spelt

17

money in capital letters.

A few feet away, lounging against one of the hotel balcony posts, was a tall, lean man who didn't appear to have a cent in his pockets. He wore patched and faded jeans, a check shirt and a wide-brimmed hat pushed back on his dark head. The family resemblance was unmistakable.

Approaching him, Jancy said warily: 'You must be Michael's brother.'

The man eyed her with interest. 'That's me. And you're Jancy Talliman. Right?' His eyes were vivid blue. 'Is Mike expecting you?'

'I don't think so.'

'You're a friend of his?'

Somehow she sensed this was going to be difficult. 'We knew each other — in London. He hasn't mentioned me, by name?'

Overhead the sparrows began another bout of high-pitched bird bickering. Quentin glanced up.

'Hear that? A good omen,' he said lazily. 'A profitable year ahead. When

18

they gather like this, there'll be seasons of plenty. A year of the sparrows means cash in hand, success, heart's desire, dreams come true and happy endings, all with a grain of salt. You don't have to believe that jazz, of course, but it's an old country saying . . . '

Then he looked at her again and went on: 'No, Michael hasn't mentioned you specifically. He's a dark horse. Never let's his right hand know what the left one's up to.' He grinned questioningly. 'His birds know what it's up to.'

'I am not,' Jancy said stiffly, 'one of his birds. Is he home today?'

Quentin shrugged. 'He was this morning, before I left for Canberra. Could be anywhere, now. I'm only his brother, not his keeper.'

He opened the passenger door of the low-slung car and Jancy clambered in. She hadn't meant to be short with him, but, one by one, disappointments were mounting.

Quentin climbed in beside her.

'What's your impressions of Bungalan, Miss Talliman. How does it compare with Big Ben and Carnaby Street?'

'First impressions are often false,' she said guardedly.

'It's a dump,' he said cheerfully. 'Six hundred people living in a cemetery. It hasn't changed in generations.'

Two late-model cars sped by and Quentin watched them until they were out of sight.

'Hundreds of motorists belt through here every day,' he went on. 'Thousands, at the weekends. Few of them ever stop, unless to fill up the tank at the garage or buy an ice-cream for the back-seat kiddies. Did you ever see such a morgue? Nobody cares, that's the trouble . . . '

'Do you care?' Jancy queried.

'I don't have a stake in Bungalan,' Quentin said. 'We're station people, not townfolk. But blokes like Sam Fowler have property. Look at those empty shops he owns, next to the pub.'

Obediently, Jancy looked at them,

stifling her impatience.

'Business is bad,' Quentin continued. 'Yet it shouldn't be. The dam employs a swarm of workers and their families, and the camp site isn't far away. Ten minutes if you're in a hurry.'

'Perhaps one of these days the town will start to prosper,' Jancy said, wishing he'd get a move on. 'Opportunities exist for people with initiative.'

Quentin tilted the hat over his eyes. 'The trouble is, people with initiative avoid this place like the plague.'

Conversationally, they were back where they had started.

Discomforted by the hot sun, Jancy squinted at her procrastinating companion. 'If you've nothing else to do, could we please leave now?'

His dark brows rose. 'Certainly, ma'am. Anything you say.'

Jancy gave him a stricken smile. Her anxiety, her eagerness to be reunited with Michael had erupted through the protective armour she'd worn so carefully. But, for heaven's sake, they couldn't sit there for ever, in the open sports car.

Removing his hat and dropping it to the floorboard, Quentin started the engine. 'I guess we have been dawdling long enough. And I wouldn't want an English rose to get scorched.'

They passed a white-painted post-office, a small schoolhouse set back from the road, and a dreary row of end-of-town cottages. Then the land opened out, wide and flat and summer-brown, with tall gums breaking the monotony of the grazing acres.

Quentin was a competent driver and curbed his natural predilection for speed. Striving to relax, to ease the smouldering tension within her, Jancy pretended to study the scenery. But her mind was in a turmoil and with every passing mile her nervousness and apprehensions increased.

Strange, but in retrospect Michael had been extraordinarily reticent in discussing his home and home life. They had been going together for two months before any kind of domestic picture emerged; a family portrait of his widowed mother, Helena; his sister Susan and brother Quentin. Of Irongates, the Rickwood property, handed down from father to son over four generations, she had no mental images whatever. It was simply a name, and rather stark at that.

So Jancy had conjured her own characters, and a high wall surrounding a stately home.

Breaking into her reverie, Quentin said: 'This is it,' and braked to a halt.

The high walls vanished. Instead, a barbed-wire fence marked the boundary line. Gone, too, in a moment of reality, was the envisaged entrance, impressive and substantial, that, in her own country, would have led on to spacious lawns and gardens.

The iron gates, flanked by leaning and crumbling masonry, were permanently open. Between the pillars spread a wide cattle grid; on the other side, a narrow, wheel-rutted track that curved past stray clumps of trees to the colonial house on the hillside.

Quentin pulled a packet of cigarettes from his shirt pocket.

'Disappointed?' He was more perceptive than she'd realised.

She couldn't answer. Instead she looked at him, struggling for composure and expecting mockery, but his blue eyes were clear.

'You've come a long way to see my brother,' he said quietly. 'Was it . . . it is that serious?'

'We knew each other . . . '

'Lots of girls know Michael. From Sydney to Sussex, I suspect.'

She glanced away. This was neither the place nor the time for defending Michael. She'd had enough trouble defending herself and rationalising her own actions in trailing after him, halfway around the world. Since the jet plane had taken off, that cold and misty day, she had been assailed by doubts and misgivings.

Quentin checked on his watch. 'I'll

be ready at four o'clock, for the return trip. Is that long enough?'

'I'd hoped . . . that Michael — '

'Well . . . ' Quentin half-smiled. 'Whoever drives, the car is at your disposal.'

He drove on, clattering across the cattle grid and along the rough track.

The large sprawling house was an attractive combination of nineteenth-century and modern architecture. It had a low-pitched iron roof, dazzling in the sun, and a wide front terrace, the stonework softened by tubs of flowering shrubs and geraniums. Overhead, fibre-glass panels set into semi-open roof decking filtered a soft green light on to the cushion-covered outdoor chairs and tables.

The long-legged girl who came out to meet them had urchin-cut, coppery hair and smoky-grey eyes.

'Where's Michael?' Quentin greeted.

The girl stared at Jancy with a puzzled frown. 'He went over to Peppertree. Cynthia phoned.'

Quentin turned and helped his passenger out of the sports car. 'Seems you're out of luck, Miss Talliman. Till sundown, at least. This is my kid sister, Susan; Jancy Talliman.'

'I've heard a little about you,' Jancy began tentatively. 'From Michael, when he was in London.' Then she paused, not wishing to sound trite but afraid that she did. 'I thought, for old time's sake . . . '

Brother and sister glanced at each other in silent communication. 'I'm sure,' Susan said carefully, 'he'll be delighted to see you again. Won't you come in and meet Mother?'

Jancy had the queerest, floating kind of feeling, as she walked up the half-dozen steps on to the terrace, that a door had been locked and barred; the same door she herself had regretfully shut when she had explained to Michael why she couldn't marry him. The same door she had been prepared to reopen, expecting Michael to be waiting for her on the other side.

Waiting, and still wanting her.

The feeling was a dark presentiment, grown more potent and disquieting from the moment she had stepped off the train; an intuition that warned her that Michael might not be the same man, or she the same girl, and that the magic they had once shared could have been diminished or negated by their separation.

As she led the way indoors, Susan said: 'I expect you're staying in Bungalan. We could have put you up here.'

'I'm sure,' Jancy said lightly, 'your guest-room is nicer than the Empire Hotel's Blue Room.'

Susan laughed. 'Years ago — a century, at least — it was the honeymoon suite.' Then she added, almost flippantly: 'Sorry about Michael's absence. Cynthia Meddow wanted him to look at a new horse she's considering buying. He shouldn't be too long, really.'

Helena Rickwood sat in a large,

chintz-covered wing chair, stitching at a square of tapestry. She was slim and elegant, the blue-framed spectacles complementing the delicate rinse in the grey hair, styled in the modern version of a French roll. It suited her beautifully.

'Mother,' Susan began, 'we have a visitor. Miss Jancy Talliman, from London.'

Slowly, Mrs Rickwood laid the needlework aside and looked up, her glance keen and measuring.

'You've come to see my son, my elder son?'

Jancy nodded, sensing an immediate barrier thrust up between them. The gracious tones, the fixed smile, the matriarchal welcome masked a cold suspicion that both confused and disconcerted.

'We were friendly when Michael was abroad,' Jancy explained. 'I wanted to see Canberra, and as Bungalan was so close . . . '

Not for a moment did Mrs Rickwood accept the pallid excuse. Smoothly and in firm control of the situation, she said: 'What a shame that Michael happens to be away right now. Do sit down.' She indicated a nearby chair. 'You must tell me all about yourself while Susan makes a pot of tea.'

'I'd like to hear about Jancy, too,' Susan protested.

'Make the tea, please.'

Susan stood her ground, stiff and stubborn. There was tension here, vibrating currents of resentment and rebellion, of challenged authority. The very air in this shaded sunroom, with its deep-piled carpet, potplants and expensive drapes and cane furniture, throbbed with the clash and conflict of temperament and personality.

Then, without another word, Susan tossed her head and stalked out.

'As we were saying,' Mrs Rickwood continued, her equanimity unruffled, 'how nice that you and Michael should be acquainted. But then, Michael is so popular and gathers friends wherever he goes.'

'That's true,' Jancy agreed, steeling herself. There was no warmth here, no affection, no open hospitality. 'He had a marvellous time in London. Parties, theatres, sightseeing. My Aunt Edith was very fond of him.'

'He visited your home?'

'Often, for Sunday tea. She was very frail, my aunt, and Michael used to make a fuss of her. She missed him when he left.'

Mrs Rickwood removed her spectacles and pondered a moment.

'My elder son has never lacked charm.'

'That's true,' Jancy said again. Her fixed smile was starting to hurt.

'And what brought you to Australia?'

'My aunt died,' Jancy told her, and even now there was pain in remembering the last days, the funeral and Edith's empty room. 'So . . . I resigned from my job and came out.'

'To stay — permanently?'

'I really don't know.'

'Where did you work?'

'At a dress shop, Mrs Rickwood. The Teen and Twenties, in Chelsea.'

'The rag trade?' Mrs Rickwood looked faintly shocked. 'A useful occupation, I suppose. Clothes are a necessity.'

'Sometimes they're fun,' Jancy answered.

Inside the house a telephone rang. Momentarily distracted, Mrs Rickwood turned her head and listened. 'Susan will answer it,' she remarked, and waited.

Jancy sat still, her handbag on her lap and wishing she'd never come to Irongates. Surely Mrs Rickwood didn't see her as a threat to the domestic harmony.

From a backroom came Susan's voice. 'For you, Mother.'

As Mrs Rickwood left her, Jancy glanced through the window, at the wild garden outside and oil-eroded hills beyond.

You've made a mistake, an inner voice warned her. A terrible mistake. In this house, among these people, you're too vulnerable. For a moment her resolution wavered; her face crumpled and a mist blurred the distant view.

Once there had been so much happiness and fulfilment that every single day had been a progression of joy. That she could be so in love, and loved in return, was the one fixed glow that had lighted the dark and desperate hours after she had laid Aunt Edith Talliman to rest.

Presently Helena Rickwood returned to the room and her chair. She went on: 'That was Cynthia phoning to say Michael won't be home. He's dining at Peppertree. I asked her to tell him that you called . . . '

For a few moments, conscious of Mrs Rickwood watching her, Jancy fought for composure, disappointment stinging her eyes.

'Perhaps . . . I can see him another time.'

'Of course,' Mrs Rickwood agreed. 'Now we must have that cup of tea. I can't imagine why Susan is taking so long.'

The small talk, the elaborate serving of the afternoon tea and the social pretence accompanying it stretched into a nightmare. Mrs Rickwood's main topic of conversation was her elder son and his relationship with Cynthia Meddow, whom Michael had known since childhood.

'They're marvellously well-suited, Miss Talliman. The ideal couple, actually. And Susan would make a beautiful bridesmaid.'

Susan nibbled on a biscuit. 'Don't count your chickens, Mother. They're not even engaged yet.'

Mrs Rickwood glanced at her coolly. 'That can be remedied, soon enough.'

Slouched in the driver's seat and reading a paperback, Quentin was waiting for Jancy at the front of the house.

'Hop in,' he greeted, pushing open the door. She noticed he'd put up the hood. Then, for her ears alone: 'Did they trot out the silver service and dainty chocolate mints?'

Jancy nodded. In the car she waved goodbye to his mother and sister, standing on the terrace, and as they drove away and out of sight she felt her face starting to crumple.

Don't cry, she told herself fiercely. Don't you dare cry!

Over the bumpy cattle grid and on to the bitumen road, Quentin said aggressively: 'Can't have been much of a visit for you, with Michael absent and Susan in one of her teenage rebel moods. She baits Mother to distraction.'

Jancy sighed. Was her misery so apparent? 'He was over at Peppercorn. I suppose — I should have phoned first. But I was so certain . . . he'd be home.'

'There's always tomorrow.' Quentin glanced at her obliquely, at the pale, drawn face, and as if sensing the despair and dejection, his voice grew gentle.

'Don't let Mother throw you. She's a terrible snob, you know. And, as a matchmaker, doing her damnedest to toll the wedding bells.' He smiled thinly. 'Mike could marry for love, but Peppertree is a large property, Cynthia's the only child and the apple of her old man's eye. In time to come, Irongates and Peppertree could affiliate into Irontree or Peppergates.'

Appreciating his dry humour but unresponsive to it, Jancy said: 'Thanks for telling me.'

Then Quentin asked, bluntly and directly: 'Is Mike that important? Did he promise to love and cherish you for as long as he lived — far from home?'

Stricken, she looked away, at the spacious paddocks and the tall gums. Her silence was eloquent.

'I apologise for my mother,' Quentin went on. 'She's an expert at putting people in their place, wherever she considers that place to be. Don't misunderstand. I'm very fond of the old girl. In her fashion, she's quite fond of me, too. But to see Peppergates become a reality is a dream she's nurtured for a long, long time. No bonnie English lass, or anyone else, is going to upset her schemes for the shape of things to come.'

'And Michael's schemes?' Jancy asked faintly.

'He'll tag along — if and when it suits him,' Quentin answered without malice. 'He's the son and heir. Lucky me. I do as I please. I'll never be the king of the castle. And you,' he added, 'will never be the queen.'

Jancy drew a deep breath. 'I didn't come here, from a Chelsea boutique, to wear a crown.'

'I'm sure you didn't,' Quentin said. 'But seeing you are here, this country needs all the talented people it can get. Are you any good?'

'Any good at what, Quentin?'

'Boutiquing. Why not open your own shop?'

If nothing else, he was good for a laugh, and suddenly Jancy knew that, whatever lay ahead, she had an ally, a sympathetic ear, a shoulder to lean on. In this vast, sun-drenched and lonely land she had found her first true friend.

'It takes money,' she answered.

'Do you have any?'

'Enough.'

'Well then,' he said, taking his hands from the wheel and throwing them wide. 'Many a career and a fortune have been launched on less.'

'Where would I start?'

'Sydney's no good,' Quentin told her. 'It has enough dress shops to clothe twice the population. Why not Bungalan?'

Despite herself, Jancy burst out laughing. 'You've got to be kidding.'

'No, I mean it,' he insisted. 'When you have nothing else to do, try counting the cars that pass through the village. Of course, they won't always use the detour, but for the next two years, while the dam's being built, it's the only route to the coast. And if you have something to sell that people are anxious to buy, they'll stop — with a squeal of brakes.'

He looked at her speculatively. 'Is there anyone special back home?'

There had been Aunt Edith, there

had been Michael . . .

Jancy's eyes clouded. 'I'm by myself now.'

'Then it's all settled,' Quentin said happily. 'Aren't the English supposed to be a nation of shopkeepers?'

'I'll think about it,' Jancy said.

'Don't think. Act. Dig in. Michael's not spoken for — yet. If you want him badly enough, get yourself a pair of boxing gloves and come out of your corner with the mitts up. What do you reckon?'

Ahead lay the town, the trees, the scattering of houses, the railway station. Was it only a few hours since she had first arrived here? It seemed a century.

In the vernacular, Jancy replied: 'I reckon.'

'Good girl,' Quentin said, and for the remainder of the journey, to the front of the hotel, sang loudly, happily and off-key.

2

After dinner that evening, Jancy went for a walk. Not that there was much to see or do in Bungalan. Already the village seemed buttoned up for the night. The few shops closed at noon on Saturday; only the hotel bar drew patronage to the main street.

The afternoon fiasco, with Michael's absence and the confrontation with his mother, might have daunted many other girls and, in despair, sent them packing.

But not Jancy Talliman. Disbelieving, hurt and shocked in turn by Mrs Rickwood's barely concealed rebuff, she had spent several hours in her bedroom and on the balcony, trying to rationalise the situation and searching for whatever salvage remained from the wreckage of her pride. In the end, determination and obstinacy proved stronger than humiliation.

Firstly, common sense indicated that she had to meet Michael again and learn the truth from his own lips — if his attachment to Cynthia Meddow was the truth. Intuition warned her that Mrs Rickwood would not be averse to distorting facts to suit her own ends.

Secondly, a rebellious streak in Jancy's nature refused to accept dismissal in such a peremptory fashion. Thirdly, if this was as Quentin had assured her the land of golden opportunity, it was up to herself to chart her own course.

Quentin's advice, his gentle persuasions, had been based on sound judgment. If she wanted Michael badly enough, she had to remain in the village, in close proximity to Irongates. Further, she had to devise ways and means of earning an income. The inheritance wouldn't last for ever.

As Jancy strolled along the darkening street, her mind seething, a procession of cars sped through the town. Idly she counted them, and in fifteen minutes had reached a total of twenty-four. The statistic was impressive. On that figure, hundreds of vehicles would pass — non-stop — through Bungalan on weekend excursions to the coast.

With such a mass exodus from the federal city, surely someone or something could tempt them to break the journey.

She noticed something else, too. The two-storey terrace adjacent to the hotel was on the western side, the corner premises featuring an unbroken brick wall running back along the side street.

Jancy strolled a couple of hundred yards along the highway, then turned and contemplated the untenanted block of shops. The brick wall was partly illuminated by an overhead street lamp. In its present state the bricks and mortar were drab and uninteresting, but an artist could work miracles with such an immense canvas.

Yes, the end shop had both position and possibilities. If only I had the nerve, Jancy mused. Courage and capital.

In shirt sleeves, Samuel Fowler stood outside the hotel, thumbs tucked under his braces as he took in the cool night air. 'Enjoying the sights?' he asked facetiously.

'It's a swinging town,' Jancy answered, pausing to speak.

The hotelkeeper rumbled with laughter.

'Swinging, you say? You can buy me out any time you want.'

'It's a shame,' Jancy said carefully, 'so many shops are vacant. With so much traffic . . . Motorists should be pulling in, spending money and creating employment.'

'Those shops have been empty for years,' Mr Fowler said with regret. 'You wouldn't care to rent one, by any chance?' And laughed again at the absurdity of the proposition.

Jancy half-smiled. 'How much would the landlord charge?'

Scratching his double chin, the portly Mr Fowler looked hard at her. 'I'm the landlord, and twenty dollars a week would suit me fine. What kind of business do you have in mind, Miss Talliman?'

Jancy reflected for a moment. 'Dress-making?'

Samuel Fowler almost burst his braces. This young woman had a sense of humour. Either that or she wasn't too bright.

'Making dresses in Bungalan! Girlie, you'd starve to death in a week. But I'll tell you what. Open up a sewing business and you can have the place, top and bottom, for ten dollars.'

'On a year's lease, Mr Fowler?'

'Anything you say, I'll go along. I'm a generous man.'

'I'm sure you are, and I'll think about it,' Jancy said gravely. 'It was just an idea.'

'We all get those,' Mr Fowler chuckled. 'We sure do.'

Jancy went into the vestibule. Through a doorway she saw Sigrid Vigeland, accompanied by two men, in the hotel parlour. Simultaneously, Sigrid caught sight of

Jancy. Her pretty face glowed with pleasure and she beckoned Jancy forward to join them.

As one of the men placed another chair at the table, Sigrid made the introductions. 'My brother Arnulf — Arnie for short — Harry Delaney and Jancy Talliman.'

Harry Delaney hurried off to the bar to get the newcomer a drink and Arnulf Vigeland said: 'I've heard all about you, Miss Talliman. You're English, a dress designer, and you're acquainted with Mike Rickwood.'

'I'm at a disadvantage,' Jancy told him. 'I know nothing whatever about you.'

'He's very promiscuous,' Sigrid said, nudging her brother.

Arnulf gazed at her with affection. 'Such a little tease. Sometimes I could wring her neck. I work at the dam, operating earth-moving equipment. I'm twenty-nine, unattached, and I like to play the field.'

'That shouldn't be difficult,' Jancy said, amused.

'We're off to a cabaret,' Sigrid explained. 'Would you like to join us, Miss Talliman?'

For a moment she was tempted. But it had been a long day and a not too late night was indicated. Surely Michael would get in touch with her tomorrow. If he didn't ... She brushed that distressing thought aside. He'd be bound to telephone her or drive straight in from Irongates. Or even from Peppertree, on his way home.

★ ★ ★

Sunday in Bungalan was worse than Saturday afternoon. She was awakened by the church bell and after that she had more than an hour to fill in before breakfast.

Quentin dropped by about ten-thirty. She was sitting out on the balcony, reading the Sunday papers, when she saw the red Jaguar pull up on the opposite side of the street. Quentin waved, she crossed to the railing and waved back.

'Glad you didn't return to Sydney on the early train,' he began as he joined her. 'You weren't too happy yesterday.'

'I extended the accommodation,' she told him.

He knew what was in her mind. 'Michael didn't come home last night,' Quentin said. 'He's playing in a polo match this morning. Cynthia's organised a cheer squad.'

Moved by the sympathy in his voice, she answered: 'You're a one-man cheer squad yourself. Did you make the trip in specially, just to tell me?'

He shook his dark head. 'I thought about you a lot last night. All alone, on a wild goose-chase.'

'Is that what you think it is?'

'Haven't you reached the same conclusion?'

She sighed and turned away. 'I have to see him, once would be enough, face to face. He won't even have to tell me; I'll know. A woman always knows.'

Shutters came down over his vivid blue eyes. 'You must have loved him — deeply.'

'Too deeply,' she answered. Slowly, hesitantly, she told Quentin of her Aunt Edith, of Michael's proposal of marriage, and of the legacy which had enabled her to span half the world.

When she'd finished, Quentin touched her cheek with his fingers.

'Often,' he said, 'when one door closes, another opens. Life's one long succession of doors.' He sat in one of the balcony chairs, then leaned back and uncoiled his long legs. 'It's a big place out here and the Rickwoods and the Meddows own a fair share of it. A big and empty place. But I wouldn't swap it for the city, and neither would you if you remained in the country long enough and learned to appreciate it, and love it, as I do. It needs fresh blood, fresh ideas. Why don't you start up that shop you talked about?'

'The shop *you* talked about,' she corrected.

His eyes mocked her. 'Scared?'

Jancy shrugged. Scared? Even the thought of such a venture was terrifying.

'If you're as good as I think you might be, you stand to make a small fortune. I'd help.'

'In a dress shop?' Now it was her turn to mock.

'With setting it up. The premises would have to be freshened up, a lease talked over, advertising arranged. You could do it — we could do it.'

Jancy ruefully shook her head. 'Good heavens, Quentin, I wish I had your superb confidence.'

'Maybe it'll grow, as the business grows.' Then briskly he said: 'I'm off to Sydney at daybreak. If I take Michael's utility we could load up with stores or whatever you want. Be ready at five o'clock.'

He stood up, grinning lazily. 'I must say you take a hell of a lot of convincing. If you lose your shirt, I'll give you one of mine. Take the plunge, sink or swim.'

When he had gone, pipping the horn and waving until he was out of sight, she recalled his last words. Like Aunt Edith, Quentin Rickwood had an answer for everything. While he'd been with her, the doubts and fears were shared, divided and minimised. His presence changed perspective. But alone again, she was swamped by misgivings.

If she left Bungalan, she would never see Michael again. Life without him would be life without hope and intolerable. If she stayed, then she would need work of one kind or another, and who would employ her? The sensible solution, as Quentin had already pointed out, was self-employment.

After lunch, Jancy had another caller. Arnie Vigeland bounded up the stairs two at a time and strode heavily down the hall. The Blue Room door was ajar, to catch the breeze, and his broad-shouldered bulk filled the opening.

'About taking a tour of the dam,' he began without preamble. 'I'm ready and waiting. Grab your purse and let's go.'

Arnulf, the hustler, was the last person she expected.

'It's all fixed,' he went on. 'We'll have afternoon tea and I'll show you the sights. Big deal. Come just as you are, but bring a headscarf and dark glasses. It'll be hot and dusty.'

Jancy didn't hesitate. Hurriedly, she ran a comb through her long honeyed hair, searched around for a scarf and sunglasses, and whisked up her handbag.

'How's that for instant action?'

'Worth an instant kiss,' he said. In the bear-hug of his arms she didn't have much choice.

The country was as Quentin had described it, big and wide, with rolling hills, and sheep grazing on the slopes. Big and deceptively uninhabited. Until Arnie's Land-Rover breasted yet another of the interminable hills and ahead, in an enormous dust bowl, spread the mighty base of an earthen dam.

Arnulf braked. 'That's it,' he said with pride.

From the distant view she saw a scattered township; huge buildings, prefabricated cottages and brightly-painted earth-moving plant. Wheel tracks patterned the arid ground in crisscross confusion.

'We're keeping up to schedule,' Arnulf told her, almost as if it were *his* dam. 'Three shifts a day, seven days a week. When it's finished there'll be a beautiful lake behind that wall, miles of clear blue water.'

The immensity of the scene stirred her with excitement.

Jancy asked: 'How many men are employed there?'

'Roughly seven hundred.'

'And women?'

Arnulf pointed. 'Those small asbestos cottages are for married couples. Maybe three hundred wives and double that in children. There's a school, an interdenominational school, a cafeteria for the single blokes, a canteen store. It's pretty well self-supporting.'

'Three hundred women,' Jancy mused.

And children would include teenage daughters, naturally. She kept staring at the dam site, at man and machinery reshaping the face of nature.

'How far have we come from Bungalan?'

'Twelve miles. Fifteen minutes by car. But many of the workmen and their families drive the other route, cross-country to Canberra. Bungalan has nothing to offer them.'

'It could,' Jancy said slowly. As hard as she tried to flaw Quentin's suggestion, it had merit and potential. If she really rented a shop, painted it externally in colours so vivid and outrageous that travellers would be half-blinded a mile away, if she stocked chic and original clothes, if she could build up a reputation based on her own fashion sense . . .

But, really, there was little profit in day-dreams. To start up a business meant planning, preparation and gambling.

Arnulf let out the clutch and drove

on down the slope. Fine red dust swirled in choking clouds, and Jancy covered her face with the chiffon scarf.

Three trucks went by, red choking dust billowing from under the wheels.

'We'd better get indoors,' Arnulf said. 'These hot, windy days are often unbearable.'

He parked outside the canteen, a building the size of an aircraft hangar.

'This is the trading post,' Arnulf explained, as he escorted her up the front steps. 'Everything from a darning needle to a frozen pecan pie.'

'Dresses, too?' Jancy asked, as the thought occurred to her.

'I guess so. Take a look for yourself while I buy a pack of cigarettes.'

In a far corner stood a free-standing rack with perhaps thirty dresses crammed front to back. Separating them and choosing a shift with fabric that interested Jancy, she held it out and with an experienced eye examined the workmanship.

It was a poor-quality garment, she realised, and overpriced at the ten dollars marked on the tag. One by one, she examined other dresses and found most of them wanting, for one reason or another.

If this is the best that's offering, she reasoned, the dress section of the canteen could do with a bit of competition; a boutique, for instance, offering style, fashion and value for money.

Arnulf returned to her side. 'Well,' he grinned, 'see anything you like?'

Jancy said frankly: 'I wouldn't buy any of them. It's poor-quality merchandise.'

'Could be,' Arnulf agreed, 'but it's also a matter of convenience. Canberra's fifty miles away, a fair hop just to pick up a new outfit.'

'Bungalan's only twelve miles.'

'So what? Where's the dress shop there?'

Jancy gave him an enigmatic smile. Bit by bit, facts and figures were presenting a clear-cut picture; a balance sheet of profit and loss, of possible success or failure. Even so, she was still reluctant to commit herself to a venture which, through ignorance of trade and local conditions, could end in financial ruin.

Changing the subject, Arnulf peered through a nearby window at the distant dam wall.

'I reckon you've seen enough for one afternoon. It's hotter and dirtier up there, over the hump, even with the lake building up. How about a drink?'

Jancy expected to be taken to a bar, or a beer garden; some place where liquor was served. Instead, Arnulf drove her to a small hut, situated in the midst of a score of identical prefabricated huts known as portables.

Inside the sparsely furnished hut he produced a bottle of whisky and another of water. She would have preferred a long, cold lemonade or even a shandy, but she knew how to hold a drink, to handle it without giving offence to the host.

She sipped the drink, the spirit barely

wetting her lips, and grimaced. It was much too strong for her unaccustomed taste.

'Well,' he said, grinning. 'I can see you're not crash hot on good whisky. Don't waste it.' And took it from her. Then, completely matter-of-fact, he added: 'How would you like to be my best girl?'

Jancy looked at him, startled. Then she said, carefully, and weighing the words: 'I'm complimented, Arnie. Truly I am. But — as you asked a direct question, I'll give a direct answer. I simply haven't the time or inclination for romantic entanglements. I'm totally committed to the shop, to staff I propose to employ, to a depressing overdraft . . . '

She smiled ruefully. 'Besides, I've been in this country such a short while. I must keep a clear and level head.'

'There's someone else.'

It was a statement, an accusation. She glanced away and paused too long before denying it.

'In England?' Arnie probed. 'In Sydney? Or here in Bungalan?'

She forced a laugh. 'None of your business, my friend.' She stood up. 'Good heavens, Arnie. A third degree on my private life? You're very cheeky. I only met you last night. Talk about fast workers in Australia . . . '

'It did occur to me,' he admitted, 'you might be the old-fashioned sort of girl. I'm not sorry you are. But I envy the bloke who has staked the claim.'

'I haven't been claimed, Arnulf.'

'You're not fooling me, Jancy Talliman. I recognise stars in the eyes when I see them shining. I've been around.'

He reached out and clasped her hands. 'A kiss to seal a friendship? One for the road?'

She was prepared to make that kind of compromise. 'Yes, Arnie. One for the road.'

As their lips met she closed her eyes. He held her gently, but his mouth hinted at bridled passion and the kiss lingered. All at once, feeling without

57

seeing, and in the darkness of her own desires, it was as if Michael were there and the kiss was his kiss. She pretended, too, that the hands holding her were Michael's hands and the face against her own Michael's face, with the attractive cleft chin and long eyelashes.

She began to tremble. This game was dangerous, and so with a shaky laugh she opened her eyes, freed herself from Arnie's embrace and stepped back.

'I need some air,' she said. 'It's very humid in here.'

'And I need a cold shower,' he murmured. He took her by the arm; in silence they walked from the hut to the Land-Rover.

Jancy did not talk much on the drive home. The diversion with Arnulf had been the climax to an incredible weekend, with its emotional swinging between buoyancy and depression.

Halfway to Bungalan, Arnie said: 'You've turned quiet, withdrawn. If I've upset you . . .'

'No,' she assured him. 'I've been indulging in a little contemplation, that's all. Nothing to do with you or,' she smiled, 'that best girl offer. I'll snap out of it soon.'

'In my room,' he went on, staring straight ahead at the open road, 'that kiss. I wasn't really there, was I? I became someone else, another man.'

Her hands were locked on her lap. 'It doesn't matter.'

'That's what you're trying to tell yourself,' he answered. 'That being in love doesn't matter. Well, I guess it can or it can't. But I can see it's a problem. I don't know much about your personal life, Jancy, but since you've moved into these parts and need a broad shoulder you can depend on me, as a friend. If I step out of line, offend you unintentionally, just yell or tread on my toes. I'll get the message.'

Glad the sunglasses she wore hid the tears that gathered, Jancy looked at him in mute gratitude. She would need all the true friends she could muster; the world was a lonely place.

In a semi-enclosed courtyard at the rear of the Empire Hotel, Samuel Fowler, barefooted, dressed in singlet and bloomer-sized khaki shorts, was watering the fernery with its many staghorns and potted plants. Before Jancy could avoid him and slip upstairs, he had noticed her arrival and turned off the hose.

'Miss Talliman,' he called, lumbering after her. 'Have you made up your mind yet about renting the shop?'

For a moment she was tempted to keep on going, to pretend she hadn't heard him. But that would have been ungracious. Instead, she turned and answered: 'I've been so busy . . . Is someone else interested in a lease?'

'Not right now,' he hastened to assure her. 'But things change from one day to the next. The unexpected can always happen.'

It had happened to her — with Michael, with Irongates. The totally, dismaying unexpected.

Jancy said frankly: 'I'd rather you didn't hustle me, Mr Fowler. I'm not even certain I could make a living here. You mustn't grasp at straws. It's only a village, all said and done.'

'True, my dear. Very true. But you did ask about the place, otherwise I wouldn't be bothering.' He poked a hand into the pocket of his voluminous shorts and pulled out a key attached to a cardboard tag.

'Why don't you take a look at the shop, and the upstairs residential. It'll be dusty, you bet, but the place could be fixed up real pretty. A woman's touch, you know . . .'

She was tired, hot and dispirited, and reluctant right then to become a target for shrewd bargaining and rough-and-ready persuasion. However, if Samuel Fuller saw her as a prospective tenant, earning him a steady income, then it might be prudent to jolly him along. She could well imagine how the ebullient hotelkeeper, with dollar signs gleaming in his eyes, pictured her in his rented shop; sitting at a sewing-machine like some Victorian spinster, and running up simple cotton dresses for simple country matrons.

'All right,' she said, deciding to play the landlord game his way. She could shower and rest later. 'Right now?'

'Better the hour, better the deed,' Mr Fowler chuckled, and led her along the street to the shop door.

The interior was larger than she'd expected, with adequate natural lighting and an abundance of cupboard and open shelf space.

In an instant her weariness and dejection dissolved and her mind, sharp and alert, began to weigh and evaluate both the premises and their potential. The wooden floor would need covering, sheer drapes on the inside of the front windows, curtains to protect the shelving, paper or paint on the discoloured walls. More elbow grease than actual cash, she decided. With economy in mind, the shop could be transformed on a shoestring budget.

Upstairs, the residential area demanded a thorough cleaning and scrubbing, but was more than adequate, in floor space, for the needs of a career girl prepared to work twelve hours a day.

Finally, praising all the obvious advantages and carefully ignoring the equally obvious disadvantages, Samuel Fowler asked bluntly for her opinion of the premises.

'They're not too bad, I suppose,' Jancy said cautiously. 'A pity the living quarters are unfurnished. That's a major problem.'

'My dear Miss Talliman,' Mr Fowler said, dismissing such a triviality with the wave of a hand. 'No problem there. Of course, I wouldn't trouble myself for everyone, but for you I'll make an exception. I'll fill the rooms with bits and pieces from the pub. A bed, a dressing-table, chairs, a mat or two. But it stands to reason I'd have to charge a little more; say, another two dollars a week.'

Jancy nodded thoughtfully. 'I must

admit that is a consideration.'

'Think hard about it,' Samuel Fowler beamed. 'The offer's open for as long as you like. Let me know by Tuesday.'

He'd make a good fisherman, Jancy thought wryly. I'm on the hook. He knows it and he knows I know it. It would be foolish to underestimate the man's shrewd capacity for business dealings, or double-dealings.

'Well, thank you,' Jancy said at length, the inspection having concluded. 'It was kind of you to show me over.'

'To be honest,' the hotelkeeper said with a self-conscious admission, 'we could do with a little dressmaker in Bungalan. Besides, I'm a widower, and none too hot with a needle and thread. Any time I wanted a button sewn on, a patch put on a shirt . . . you'd be mighty handy. I'd pay, naturally.'

'For the landlord's buttons,' Jancy replied, matching his self-proclaimed generosity, 'there'd be no charge.'

Back at the Empire, Mr Fowler resumed

the watering and Jancy returned to the Blue Room. For a few minutes she lay on the bed, trying to relax. She had an hour to fill in before dinner, an empty hour, and all at once a shroud of melancholy enveloped her.

Where was Michael now, she wondered miserably. Why hadn't he phoned her, or called to see her? How could she plan tomorrow or the next day or next week or even next month without the assurance that he still loved her, still wanted her.

'Oh, Michael,' she whispered silently to the lonely room. 'Tell me if it's too late. Tell me if I've lost you.'

★　★　★

Quentin Rickwood was sprawled in a deckchair, a can of beer in one hand, a racing-car magazine on his lap, when Michael, with a deliberate squeal of tyres, brought the station utility to a halt at the front steps.

Bounding up on to the terrace,

Michael casually gave a thumb-up signal in greeting.

'It's damned hot,' he said, mopping his face. 'Any more cans on the ice?'

'Unless we have a secret drinker in the family,' Quentin answered lazily, 'about a dozen. How was the weekend?'

'Fine. We won the polo game.'

'Bully for you. And Cynthia? Who's winning her game?'

Michael ignored the innuedo. Will I tell him, Quentin mused. Then said: 'I've got news for you. We've had a visitor.'

At that precise moment, spoiling the calculated effect, the telephone rang and Michael started for indoors.

'Don't go,' Quentin called after him. Too sharply.

Michael paused, swung round and titled his dark head questioningly to one side. He stared coolly at his younger brother. 'The call could be mine.'

'Wait till you hear what I have to say.'

'Whatever it is, it can wait. I need a drink.'

As he began to walk into the house, Susan hurried out and met him halfway. 'Well, well,' she said with exaggerated surprise. 'Big brother returns from his wild weekend.'

'You ought to grow up and try one or two yourself,' Michael growled.

'And fall pregnant?' Susan pulled a face. 'No, thanks. I'll stay virginal and virtuous.'

'Never been propositioned?' Michael frowned. 'We can't all be perfect, baby doll.'

Susan tossed her head. 'Someone seems to think you are. Jancy Talliman. Remember her? She wants to speak with you.'

Watching for reaction with half-shut eyes, Quentin observed the shockwave ripple across Michael's dark face.

'She's here? On the telephone?'

Susan nodded, enjoying the drama on hand. Smugly she said: 'Yesterday she was here. Right now she's in Bungalan.'

Without another word, Michael swept past her.

Susan looked down at Quentin. 'Shall we join the fun?'

Quentin got up from the deckchair. 'After you, my girl. We've had the overture. I wouldn't miss the first act.'

Together they followed their brother into the living room, where Helena Rickwood was arranging bowls of flowers.

'Why the sudden interest in Michael's affairs?' she demanded. 'His telephone conversations should be private.'

'Then we'll all go outside,' Susan said sweetly. 'You too, Mother.'

Testily Michael made a rough gesture to the family to hold their respective tongues. Grinning at each other and ignoring their mother's stern-faced disapproval, Quentin and Susan sat back to enjoy the proceedings.

'I've only just come in,' Michael was saying, deliberately turning his back on them. 'Yes, I was away for the weekend, but I'm sure we can manage a get-together. How long will you be staying there?'

He paused and rubbed the back of his neck. 'That's fine. It's wonderful, hearing from you again. I'll call in as soon as possible, but it can't be tonight, I'm afraid. Another engagement. I'd gladly put it off, but it would be rather awkward . . . '

He turned and looked at his mother, seemingly intent upon her floral arrangements, and went on: 'You'll be at the hotel tomorrow night? Well, that's splendid. We can crack open a bottle of champagne to celebrate. I'll save the news until then. All right, Jancy. Goodbye.'

Slowly he cradled the receiver, then stood staring down at it in brief contemplation.

'Tomorrow night,' Mrs Rickwood said in her precise and formal manner, 'I'd planned to have the Meddows over to dinner.'

'You can't beat this instant planning,' Susan chortled. 'You'll have to make it Tuesday night, Michael.'

'Tuesday's out,' Michael said stiffly. 'I have to go into Canberra. It's the monthly polo club meeting.'

'Then how about Wednesday?' Quentin said brightly. 'If you stall long enough, she'll have returned to Sydney. With a bit of luck, she might even be on her way back to London, removed from your life for ever.'

A flush darkened Michael's deeply tanned face. 'Why don't you mind your own bloody business?'

'That's right,' Susan said, waving an admonishing finger at the younger brother. 'Any friend of Michael's isn't necessarily a friend of yours, Quentin.'

Mrs Rickwood thumped the table. 'I won't hear any more of this ridiculous talk. It's all very difficult. If Michael doesn't want to get involved with this girl, whoever she is, or renew an old acquaintance, then he'll have to be quite firm. Whatever their relationship in the past, it's none of our concern. Michael has other commitments and responsibilities. He's been back from abroad now for months and months, and not a mention of this Miss Talliman.'

She carried a bowl of flowers to the buffet. 'Besides, there's Cynthia to consider.'

'Good old Cynthia,' Susan sighed, and passing Quentin on her way out of the room, tousled his hair.

'The best thing,' Mrs Rickwood went on, ignoring her daughter's departure, 'would be for this girl to realise she has no future here. I must say, it's rather odd that she travelled such a distance to see you.'

Michael shrugged. 'Well, we met in London. I think I'll call her back and make it Wednesday night. The least I can do is spend a couple of hours with her before she leaves town.'

'Perhaps,' Quentin said blandly, 'she won't be leaving town.'

'Nonsense,' his mother retorted crisply. 'There's nothing to keep her in Bungalan.'

Quentin got to his feet. His mother could be such a snob. 'I guess Michael will have to sort out his own involvements. Is Cynthia aware of the competition?'

'Quentin!' Mrs Rickwood's voice was coldly authoritative. 'That's enough. Stop needling Michael. Competition, indeed! Go off and do whatever you have to do, while we have a talk. Tomorrow night Cynthia and her father are coming to dinner.'

Quentin shook his head. 'Don't set a place for me. I'm going to Sydney first thing in the morning. In the ute, on business. I'll be gone all day and half the night.'

'That's too bad,' his mother said. 'If you're not here, then you're not. It can't be helped.'

Some things can't, some things can, Quentin reflected as he returned to his magazine and terrace chair. All of a sudden he felt sorry for Jancy Talliman, the unwanted mustard in a Rickwood-Meddow ham sandwich.

But at first light, when he pipped the horn and Jancy came out of the hotel, he did not feel the least bit sorry for her. In her candy-pink shoes, pink sheath dress and beige make-up, the girl from London was a knockout.

'I wasn't sure you'd be coming,' Quentin said for openers, as Jancy climbed in beside him. Strain shadowed her face.

'I wasn't sure myself,' she answered, settling herself for the long journey ahead.

'What decided you? The phone calls from Michael?'

'You were there? You heard?'

The decision had been made for her, in Michael's circumspection, in the manner of his greeting. Not for a moment had she been deceived by the forced enthusiasm. He had been caught off-guard, embarrassed — with his family, no doubt, watching him and listening to his every word.

Half the night Jancy Talliman had lain awake, wondering whether to pack her bag and leave on the morning train or to follow Quentin's advice; to dig her own foundations in this country village and to build a new and rewarding life for herself.

Quentin leaned close to her. 'You seem tired, Jancy. We'll be travelling for hours, so why don't you lean on me and have a nap.'

'I'm perfectly all right,' she said.

In ten minutes she was asleep, her head resting heavily on his shoulder. How vulnerable she is, he thought, looking down at her and catching the subtle fragrance of the perfume she wore. You're going to need a strong arm in Bungalan, Miss Talliman, and mine's as good as any. Don't depend on Michael.

The morning was clear and clean, polished by the early morning sun. The road was deserted and as he sped along, through wide and yellow pasturelands, Quentin hummed a happy tune.

Methodically, Jancy had made a list and knew exactly what had to be bought. On the other hand, with intimate knowledge of Sydney, Quentin knew exactly where to buy.

Once they arrived, the day passed at

express speed. Jancy checked out of the private hotel where she'd been staying and Quentin stowed her luggage under the canopy in the back of the utility. She went to the bank, withdrew a sum of money and had the balance transferred to a branch in Canberra. Then the shopping and bargaining began.

'We'll buy nothing at retail prices,' Quentin told her. 'The important thing is to get the most for the least. By scouting around and making comparisons, you'll save a helluva lot of dollars.'

She needed a heavy-duty sewing-machine, and Quentin took her to premises that sold reconditioned models at half-price. She bought curtain material and rolls of wallpaper, of superseded designs, at throw-out prices in a basement sale. And gallons of paint and odd lengths of broadloom carpeting at a bankruptcy disposal centre.

Item by item was scored from the list, and by four-thirty that afternoon the utility was stacked as high as the cabin roof.

As well as the furnishings, hardware and sewing-machine, Quentin had directed her to a warehouse where she had hand-picked a hundred assorted dresses. Fifty of these had been a cash sale, the balance on a bi-monthly account.

The dresses were absurdly cheap, last year's stock, but in showroom condition. One by one Jancy had chosen each garment, realising instinctively with her training, knowledge and flair for design how they could be given the London mod look.

They spent two hours at the warehouse and Quentin was hard put to conceal his boredom and impatience.

She bought other things, too; evening bags made in Hongkong, a line of Japanese purses and handbags, a bulk deal in Indian ear-rings and scarves, belts, Bermuda socks, and odds and ends such as braiding, ribbons and buttons.

Then, mentally and physically exhausted, they were heading back to Bungalan,

through the city's thinning outer sub-
urbs and into open country, hilly and
thickly wooded.

Jancy had kicked off her shoes and
was slouched against the seat. 'For
better or worse,' she announced, 'I've
spent close on a thousand dollars.'

Quentin chuckled. 'Not really. You
have assets. Think positively. If things
came to the worst you could always sell
the sewing-machine.'

Her pale smile was fleeting. 'You
think it will come to that? The worst?'

'I reckon you'll do just fine,' Quentin
said, and resisted a crazy impulse to
bring the utility to a stand-still and take
Jancy Talliman in his arms. He'd never
before met anyone quite like this girl.

She slept soundly on the journey
home. Halfway, Quentin pulled into an
all-night roadside café frequented by
truck drivers on the interstate haul, and
they had a light meal.

So it was almost ten o'clock before
they reached the Empire Hotel. As
Quentin turned the truck into the main

street and pulled up outside, Arnulf and Sigrid emerged from the front entrance.

'There you are . . . ' Sigrid cried, running across the footpath. 'You've been gone all day,' she added anxiously. 'I was so worried . . . '

Jancy climbed stiffly from the vehicle and stretched her limbs.

'Quentin took me to Sydney,' she explained. More than anything else in the world she wanted to crawl into bed and stay there for a week, but the loose ends of the day had yet to be tied.

While Quentin went in search of Samuel Fowler to get the key of the end shop and unload the utility, Jancy told Sigrid of her plans to open a boutique.

'I'll need assistance, Sigrid, and if you'd like a job, then we'll talk about it tomorrow.'

The blonde Norwegian hotel maid gave a whoop of joy and hugged her brother.

'In a boutique! Oh, Miss Talliman, all my life I've wanted to do that kind of work.'

Arnuld put an arm affectionately around Sigrid's shoulders. 'Why not? Live dangerously.' Then, to Jancy: 'We were just on our way back to Warabee. Sigrid has the day off tomorrow and intended spending it with her mother.'

'I wish I were having the day off,' Jancy said fervently. 'But I have to start on the shop, scrubbing and cleaning, ready for decorating. I'd like to open on Saturday.'

Sigrid glanced quickly at her brother for affirmation. 'Mother won't mind. I'd like to help, too.'

'How many hired hands would you need?' Arnulf asked.

'I'd like a dozen,' Jancy told him, 'but it's out of the question. I couldn't afford to pay them.'

'I'm not talking about paying,' Arnulf said. 'I could round up five or six mates. Could you use them?'

The offer was overwhelming. She wanted to thank him, but her throat closed up. Quentin, Sigrid, Arnie and half a dozen voluntary workers. What

79

couldn't they accomplish in a single day?

Slowly, in wordless gratitude, she put a hand on his arm. She smiled and he smiled back, and then her smile twisted into a grimace and tears were streaming down her cheeks.

'It's too much,' she wept. 'It's just . . . too much.'

'Please, Miss Talliman,' Sigrid said, trying to comfort her. 'Don't cry. It's going to be fabulous, real whizzy. Arnie's friends will do anything in the world. It's true. There hasn't been a bit of excitement in Bungalan for the last century and now you're here, with swinging ideas, and everyone's racing about . . . Please don't cry . . . '

They had all gone their diverse ways. Arnulf Vigeland had assisted in the unloading, Sigrid had returned the shop key and now Jancy was alone, bone-weary yet filled with a throbbing exultation.

It was cool on the front balcony and the night air refreshed her. How quiet the town was. Not a single passing car disturbed the midnight silence. She stood by the wrought-iron railing looking out through the darkness, at the black hump of the church and the bell-tower, at the shops and the slumbering houses, at the myriad stars overhead.

You've gone and done it, Jancy Talliman, she told herself, and even now, having done it, the whole thing seemed unreal, unbelievable in retrospect.

But Aunt Edith would have approved. Aunt Edith would have applauded her determination, fortitude and courage.

Out there were Irongates and Michael. The man she loved, the only man she had ever loved.

You'll be proud of me, she thought. You'll be glad I'm here, in Bungalan. I'll make you glad.

3

The rag trade, Mrs Rickwood had called it, with superiority and conde- scension. Clothes were a necessity. But then, the English were renowned for being a nation of shopkeepers.

Jancy remembered this wounding barb of social inequality as she unlocked the front door of the shop. But the arrogance of the remark, from a country woman in the fleece trade, no longer riled. The thorn had not been deep enough to fester.

On the contrary, in retrospect Jancy could almost smile at their confronta- tion. Measure for measure, Mrs Rickwood and the newcomer to Bungalan were each fully aware of the other.

The rag trade . . . Whatever it was called by those who wished to demean the industry, Jancy was determined her boutique would be a cut above the average shop supplying women's wearing apparel. Having made a decision and acted upon it, she was now up to her neck in accumulated creditors, stock and business worries.

Would she sink, or swim? The clothing industry was deep and wide, and many, she knew, had foundered through lack of funds and through inexperience.

All her new-found friends, however, had rallied with voluntary labour, encouragement and moral support. So she wasn't paddling alone. It was a warming, wonderful feeling to know that others cared for her and about her.

'Well, what do we do first?' Sigrid asked, unable to conceal her excitement. The shop was ready, the stock attractively displayed. Everything was new and elegant.

'Wait for the first customer, of course,' Jancy told her. 'Without them we're not even in business.'

It was exactly two o'clock on the Saturday afternoon. How so much work had been accomplished in such a short space of time still remained a mystery, one which Jancy would never be able to fathom. But, by diverse means, working day and night and often late into the early hours, the premises had been remodelled and decorated and the stock unpacked and price-tagged.

The interior featured soft carpet, free-standing racks of clothes, a couple of glass-topped counters on rollers, wall units and shelving. Sheer apricot-coloured curtains were draped at the windows overlooking the street, and half a dozen secondhand manikins strategically placed here and there were dressed in Jancy's own creations.

The inside of the shop was most impressive. But outside Jancy had gone overboard to concentrate on shock advertising. If you want to be heard, she had decided, beat a big drum.

Enough to give anyone a migraine, Quentin had commented at first sight of the outside décor. And he was right, for it served the purpose. The incredible whorls of vivid colour that clothed the previously bare brickwork of the end wall of the premises would be seen, on a clear day, practically for ever.

The paintwork was a signwriter's nightmare, guaranteed to give anyone a headache who stared at it too long.

'That's exactly the point,' Jancy had told Quentin. 'I want it to stun people. I want motorists who might have intended passing on to stop and gape. Once they've stopped, a woman's natural curiosity is bound to take over. At least, that's my line of reasoning. Only time will tell if I'm right or wrong.'

Quentin had been standing several hundred yards along the street and he'd gaped, his expression one of painful disbelief.

'Who did it? Who created such a monstrosity?'

'One of Arnie Vigeland's friends. An amateur artist.'

The psychedelic reds, greens, oranges, purples and blues flowed and melted into each other in a kind of Dali daze.

'Amateur's the word,' Quentin agreed. And slipped on his sunglasses to diminish the distraction.

'I really like it,' Jancy said, approving the paintwork. 'It's instant vulgarity. Travellers will see this enormous hotch-potch of colour a mile off, and when they get closer they'll focus on Sigfrid's effort.'

Sigrid's contribution to the blinding paint job was a large calico banner strung across and above the front of the shop premises in the main street. It read, in huge print: 'For the tops in fashion. JANCY'S. Preview opening Saturday 2 p.m.'

Appraising the sign, Quentin asked, poker-faced: 'What about the fashionable bottoms?'

'We supply those, too,' Jancy told him with a giggle. 'Now run along and spread the glad tidings among your girl friends. For the gala day it will be first come, first served.'

'When you put in a line of men's

handkerchiefs,' Quentin said, 'I might start being a regular customer.'

The twin front doors were wide open, inviting patronage. By three o'clock Jancy had sold a silk scarf to Miss Mason, Bungalan's elderly postmistress, a fifteen-dollar shift dress to a teenager who lived in the street behind the hotel, and an Italian tooled leather belt to the wife of the grocery store owner. But a portion of the sales was a kind of charity, as Jancy was uncomfortably aware.

Samuel Fowler had called in briefly to wish her well and to count the heads. Though he did not state it in as many words, it was obvious he had the continuity of his shop rent foremost in mind.

At three-thirty, with Jancy starting to feel a little sick with tension and disappointment, a car pulled up out front and a woman got out of the passenger seat.

Peering through the front curtains, Sigrid whispered: 'Here's a likely one.'

And beckoned Jancy forward. 'From Canberra, I'll bet.'

The woman was in her late thirties, tall and slim, and dressed simply but, to Jancy's practised eye, expensively. As she strolled into the boutique, Jancy approached the potential customer with a welcoming smile.

'Can I help you, Madam?'

'That depends,' the woman said, very casual and noncommittal. 'I'd prefer, for now, just to look around.'

'By all means. If you wanted something for a special occasion it can be designed and made up for you here in the boutique.'

'That's interesting.' The woman began to thaw slightly. 'When I saw that sign — your sign — I couldn't resist asking my husband to stop for a few minutes. We're on our way to the coast.' She glanced about. 'You appear to have nice things.'

The woman was still browsing among the goods on display when Susan Rickwood came in, her pretty, young face alight with a glow of pleasure.

'Hello, Jancy,' she greeted, a trifle guardedly, Jancy thought, and with a friendly nod to Sigrid. 'Tried to get here sharp on two, for the official opening, but Mother . . . ' She shrugged. 'How's business?'

Jancy made a church steeple with her hands. 'You can see for yourself. It's hardly Selfridges on sale day.'

'It's still early, so don't despair. Quentin's talked of nothing else but what you've been doing here. It's fabulous, Jancy. Absolutely terrific. The transformation is quite unbelievable.' Jancy wasn't sure whether she was being loudly ecstatic for the benefit of the sole customer in the shop. 'Do you have anything that might suit me?'

Jancy gave a wan smile, heartened a little by Susan's infectious enthusiasm. While doing her best to disguise it, Jancy's depression was increasing with every passing minute. Had she badly miscalculated? Expected too much too soon?

'Yes,' she said. 'Several things, I'm sure, are your cut and style. I had you in mind when I chose them.'

The girl swung left and right, all eyes, anxious to check along the racks. 'How can I curb my natural extravagance?'

'Easy,' Jancy suggested drily. 'By paying cash. Then what you don't have you can't spend.'

Susan laughed. 'I have a better way. Just keep remembering I'm saving to go abroad — dollar by dollar. A long-range plan. I'll make it in about three years, if I'm lucky, but I'm determined to get there.'

There was a commotion out in the street and Jancy moved swiftly to the doorway. A car had screamed noisily round the corner and was braking with a squeal of tyres. Behind it came another car, and another — three cars, five cars, a motorcade of ten, fifteen vehicles crowding the roadway.

Sigrid ran outside, took one startled look at the newcomers and turned to Jancy.

'They're from Warabee dam,' she cried, her eyes sparkling. 'My mother, all her neighbours and friends . . . They've come . . . they're here for the grand opening. Oh, how wonderful!'

She hadn't finished speaking before the crowd of people enveloped them. Leading more than a score of females, young and middle-aged, and a number of men, Mrs Vigeland trailed into the shop.

Susan grabbed Jancy's arm. 'How on earth are you going to cope with this mob? You can't serve twenty people at one and the same time.'

'Who cares?' Jancy retorted with reckless abandon. 'They'll wait, take their turn. Have you ever worked in a shop?'

Susan shook her head.

'Too bad,' Jancy said crisply. 'You're hired for the rest of the afternoon. Let's sell every woman on the premises a new dress. Or at least a pair of pantyhose.' Then, over her shoulder as she hurried away, 'Two dresses, if you think they can afford it.'

Jancy Talliman closed the boutique at sundown, exhausted and triumphant. The takings exceeded her wildest expectations. Seventeen dresses, including a navy-blue and white ensemble to the woman from Canberra. Several handbags, half a dozen belts, at least forty pairs of cut-price pantyhose, and promises by many of the purchasers to 'come again soon'.

She lay on the bed in the upstairs flat that evening, watching the white curtains hanging motionless in the heat.

Aunt Edith would be pleased, she ruminated sadly, the old lady never far away in memory. If she'd been here today, watching and listening, bolstering me with her courage and wisdom . . .

But Aunt Edith was gone, and love could recall her only in part. Still, her spirit lingered and that ensured she would never be forgotten.

How would Aunt Edith have reacted, Jancy mused, a shadow crossing her face at the recollection, to the unexpected arrival of Cynthia Meddow that afternoon.

Jancy had had an armful of dresses, hastening from racks to fitting-rooms, trying to serve half a dozen at the same time — an impossible task — when Susan cornered her.

'Guess what. Lady Peppertree has just strolled in,' she whispered theatrically.

Jancy stared at her blankly, her mind on a score of other more pressing things.

'Peppertree?' Her brow furrowed; she had neither the time nor the temper for youthful guessing games.

'Cynthia,' Susan explained in a rush. 'Cynthia Meddow. Michael's Cynthia. She's here.'

Michael's Cynthia . . . That summed it up beautifully. If the shock registered, Susan failed to notice. Jancy swung round, peering among the women in the shop, her unfitted, half-undressed customers momentarily in limbo.

Cynthia — the young woman Jancy presumed was Lady Peppertree, stood inside the doorway, glancing to left and right, pleasant surprise at the sight of the bustling crowd widening her eyes. She was tall and slender with dark brown hair cut short and a strong, mobile jaw. Self-assured and attractive, she permeated country health and vitality as she stood, in an indolent pose, one hand on her hip, the other pressed in amusement against her cheek.

So that's Michael's fiancée, Jancy thought, fully prepared to dislike her immediately. That's the girl for whom a marriage is being arranged. A union of properties, wealth and countless acres of land.

But surely Michael wouldn't accept his mother's interference in so personal a decision. Matriarch or not, surely Michael wouldn't allow her to run his life. This was Australia, not southern Europe where marriage-making had been an accepted practice for centuries past.

'Miss Talliman . . . ' Sigrid leaned over the glass counter. 'That red-and-white knitted suit you're carrying. A girl's in there waiting to try it on. You told her you'd bring it in immediately . . . '

Jancy shook her head, trying to clear it. Too much was happening too fast and she was unprepared for it.

'I was interrupted,' she said. 'Here, Sigrid, take the lot.' She thrust the armful of dresses at her astonished assistant.

Before Jancy could make any further move, Cynthia Meddow was standing before her.

'Cynthia,' Susan was saying, making formal introduction, 'this is Jancy Talliman, who owns the boutique. Jancy, Cynthia Meddow, from Peppertree . . . '

Cynthia's smile was open and friendly. 'I hope you do very well here. The new shop, and all the work you've done, is the talk of the district. Quentin's a good public relations man; I'd certainly cultivate him. Would you have anything in my size, Miss Talliman? I'm all for supporting local trade, and you appear to have lots of lovely things.'

So she hadn't been able to dislike Cynthia Meddow after all. The young woman was charming and uncomplicated, a really nice person.

Jancy closed her mind to Cynthia — the tag of Lady Peppertree was not only uncharitable, but unfair — and to the problems of the shop. No use worrying over one or the other. For better or worse she had elected to set down roots in Bungalan, the boutique was launched, and Jancy Talliman had become a business woman.

At irregular intervals cars sped past in the main street outside. There were raised voices and loud laughter from the direction of the Empire Hotel.

Jancy was still on the bed, half-asleep and reminding herself she'd have to get up soon and prepare a meal, when, as if from a great distance, she heard a loud knocking.

'Open up, Jancy. I want to talk to you. Open up.'

The words were blurred and the identity of the voice did not register. In a state of lethargy she stumbled across to the window, pushed it higher and poked her head out. 'Who's down there?'

'Come and see for yourself.'

Was it Quentin, whom she had half-expected to call in that afternoon? For a moment she had half a mind to tell him she was too tired to take a rain check on the visit, but a sense of responsibility prevailed. The debt she owed was too great for such offhand behaviour.

Indirectly, Quentin had helped bring the day's success to fruition. Had he not persuaded her to stay in Bungalan, accompanied her to Sydney, spread the word of her gala opening around the district . . . ?

Jancy gave a rueful laugh. 'I'll be right there,' she called, and went down the stairs to open up.

As she unbolted the front door she began: 'It's Saturday evening. Why aren't you out with your friends, at the hotel or in Canberra. It's a night for celebrating . . . '

Her voice tailed off in midstream. She looked up at him, the single shop light she had switched on reflecting the sheen of his thick black hair, his tanned and handsome face.

She had been prepared for Quentin, but not for this man.

'Oh, it's you.'

Michael Rickwood eyed her lazily. 'You're disappointed? Someone else, perhaps?'

She felt a nerve in her jaw quiver, a flush mounting her cheeks. So nonchalant, as if he had turned the clock back to Kensington, as if the past months of grief and misery and past weeks of ignoring her, neglecting her, did not exist.

Jancy took a long, deep breath. 'No — on both counts. I was resting, that's all. It was an incredible, hectic afternoon . . . ' Then, struggling to regain her composure, despising and adoring him simultaneously in a fierce emotional wrenching, she went on: 'Why did you bother to come?'

'To wish you luck, belatedly I'm afraid, on your venture. I've been in Queensland. Only got back a few hours ago.' He held out a bottle of champagne. 'I brought this — to toast the opening of Jancy's boutique.'

'You're a trifle late,' she said. 'The grand opening terminated several hours ago.'

Michael gave her a lopsided grin and cleared his throat.

'I apologise. As I said before, I was hundreds of miles away, at stock sales in Brisbane. I left the day after I spoke to you on the phone. It was pre-arranged — air tickets, accommodation. I couldn't be in two places at once, you must realise that. Besides, you gave me no warning that you were coming here. Simply dropped in, out of the blue . . . '

Her back ached and an infuriating lump rose in her throat. 'That's true,' she admitted.

'Well then, here I am,' Michael said

persuasively. 'And that's the main thing. To welcome you to Bungalan. Aren't you going to invite me in?'

Jancy stared at him, still rebellious, unforgiving. 'Is there any reason why I should?'

His expression grew stern. 'I can think of half a dozen. That you love me, for one. I want to talk to you. I just want to sit down, drink the bubbly and talk.'

Jancy leaned against the door jamb. 'We could have talked a week ago, two weeks. You could have phoned, or written. You could have called in when passing. You must have passed through the town at one time or another.'

She sounded petulant, but was past caring. He had hurt her deeply and might as well know it.

'I wanted to come — and that's the truth. But I have a job to do at Irongates. Surely you can understand that.'

She felt chilled from a contained anger. 'I suppose I do.'

'From the way you said that, I'm sure you don't. Look,' he went on crisply. 'The last time we were face to face, it was twelve thousand miles away, on the other side of the world. I wanted to marry you, but you couldn't, or wouldn't, leave your responsibilities, your Aunt Edith. You're not Robinson Crusoe, Jancy. You're not the only person committed to something by circumstance.'

Grudgingly she conceded that, her hostility starting to evaporate. His presence, his nearness was weakening all her firm intentions.

And Michael sensed her wavering. 'Things change, Jancy. People change. When we were together in London . . . that was one thing. When we separated, when I returned home, I thought I would never see you again. You were caring for your aged aunt, I was here caring for our property. It's as simple as that.'

Slowly, Jancy drew herself up to her full height. 'Nothing is *that* simple,' she said coolly. 'Day after day I waited for you, for a message. I even went to Irongates and that was a great reception, too.'

A broad grin twisted his mouth. As if speaking to a recalcitrant child, he said patiently: 'Calm down; there's so much I want to tell you. But certainly not out here, on the footpath. Do you want to make your private business public?'

He was trying to jolly her along, and she was in no mood for jollying.

'I was under the impression it was public,' she retorted. 'In your family circle, at least.'

For a moment she hesitated, conceding the point. 'All right, Michael. But for ten minutes only.'

Upstairs, in the small living area off the bedroom, Jancy gave a shrug of apology at the condition of the flat. 'I haven't settled in up here yet. We've been concentrating on downstairs. But this will be fixed up presently.'

Glancing about, at the shabby second-hand furniture the hotelkeeper landlord had provided, and bits and pieces Jancy had acquired, at the bare floorboards, the curtain-less window with its drab brown holland blind, Michael said:

'I've no doubt you'll transform the place, if the shop is any criterion of your decorative ability. What's in here?'

He crossed to the partly-closed bedroom door, pushed it open and walked through. 'This is better. More of the feminine touch, more homely. Bring in two glasses, Jancy.'

Though she resented his intrusion, she did not protest. To force the issue of remaining in the living room would have been adolescent; besides, if she goaded him into a huffy departure they might never be reconciled.

He was sitting on the side of her bed, his brow furrowed as he patiently unwound the wiring of the champagne cork.

'We had lots of champagne in London,' he said quietly.

'I've not forgotten,' she said, handing him a napkin to wrap about the bottle.

She placed two tumblers on the bedside table, then stood back and watched her visitor. When the voice from the street had summoned her she'd switched on the bedlamp. The light was soft and intimate, an intimacy now shared with the man sitting near by, his dark head and broad shoulders in shadow.

She tried not to think about his shoulders or the physical strength that emanated from him. More disturbed by his presence than she cared to admit, she looked at her wristwatch, noticed with surprise that it was past eight o'clock, and realised she hadn't eaten since mid-morning.

'I think,' she said, 'I'd prefer a cup of tea. I'm quite hungry and on an empty stomach . . . '

'Nonsense. This will give you an appetite.'

She thought: For a meal or for you?

'There! It's done!' The cork popped and she reached for the glasses.

When they were filled he set the

bottle on the floor near the end of the bed.

'Congratulations,' he said, smiling, 'on your many accomplishments. Good cheer for Jancy's boutique.'

'All right, I'll drink to that.' And when she'd half-emptied the glass added recklessly: 'Another toast — to your engagement.'

His smile slipped and his eyes grew hard. Staring up at her, he said: 'I should have been here the first day. I feel badly about that . . .'

'I wish you had been here. I needed you, Michael. I needed you badly. I was so alone.'

'I'm sorry. I'm here now and you're no longer alone.' He held out a hand and after a brief hesitation she took it in her own.

'I've known Cynthia since child-hood,' he went on, refilling his glass. 'For the record, we're not engaged.'

'Do you propose to become engaged?' Jancy felt she had a right to be informed.

Michael shrugged. 'The Rickwoods

have been in this district for almost a century. We're part of the land. The Meddows have their land, too. Only fences divide both holdings.' He paused. 'All our lives we've been neighbours and good friends.'

Jancy sat next to him on the bed. 'She's a charming girl. I guess I'm sorry also. For being difficult, lashing out, ill-humoured.' She stared at the wine bubbles in the tumbler she held. 'It's all a bit of a mess, really. I mean . . . there was you and me, and now there's Cynthia and you . . . I flew all this way, unknowingly, unwittingly, to stir up a hornets' nest.'

He grinned briefly. 'Darling Jancy, you're dramatising. You haven't stirred up anything. You're here in innocence. But you still love me, I know.'

Was it so apparent? She was trying desperately hard not to love him. He shouldn't have said that. It sounded a little conceited.

'The question is, Michael,' she said, throwing caution to the winds, 'with whom are you in love?'

He set down the glass on the table and took her in his arms. Prudence urged her to resist, but she had dreamed of this too long. One kiss and she was sure of him again. One kiss and the old fires were rekindled. One kiss . . .

His ardour was as strong, as fierce as she remembered it.

'Oh, Michael,' she breathed in his embrace. 'We shouldn't be getting carried away. It's too complicated.'

Slowly she disengaged herself and held him at arms' length. 'I was half-asleep before and now I'm wide awake. We have to think rationally, and I can't . . . The champagne's making me float. Would you like to stay for a meal?'

'Why not? As I recall, you were an excellent cook.' Then he was on his feet, pulling her up with him. 'I'll even help prepare it.'

'Anything special you'd like?'

He shook his head and squeezed her

hand. 'Everything I like is right here, in Bungalan.'

Jancy laughed. 'Don't be too sure of yourself,' she warned him, with a laugh. As he'd told her himself, there were other things to consider — people such as Helena Rickwood and Cynthia Meddow. It was possible that Cynthia might relinquish her hold on Michael, if she became aware of his love for another woman, but Mrs Rickwood would fight grimly until the end.

And you, Jancy told herself as she filled a kettle, you can't afford to be too sure of yourself, either.

4

Jancy felt a trifle uneasy when, opening the shop for business on the following Monday morning, she found Susan Rickwood waiting outside.

Though immediately aware of the reason for the girl's presence, Jancy chose to pretend otherwise. 'Hello,' she greeted merrily. 'My first customer for the week.'

Susan's face was a study. 'Not a customer,' she protested. 'You offered me a job, remember? Two days ago, to be exact. Well, here I am. What do I do first? Sign a time book, punch a bundy? I told you I'm saving to go to Europe.'

'Neither.' Jancy gazed at her thoughtfully, regretting the foolish spur-of-the-moment gesture she had made. Was it only two days ago? It seemed like two long weeks. And in suggesting employment to Susan, what kind of crises had she triggered off in the Rickwood hierarchy?

Anxiety shadowed Susan's face. 'You haven't changed your mind?'

Jancy shrugged. If a battle was to be waged, she would need all the troops she could muster, even defectors.

'No,' she said kindly. 'I wouldn't do that to you. The job offer was made in good faith. Come on in. Sigrid should be here in a moment. She'll take your measurements and run you up a smock, a pink one, exactly the same as the one she wears.'

Business was slack that early in the morning, which provided Susan with ample time to take her employer into her confidence.

'I suppose you've been wondering about the reaction back at the homestead,' Susan began tentatively during a coffee break in the back room.

'It had crossed my mind,' Jancy admitted.

Susan wrinkled her nose. 'The balloon went up. Vesuvius erupted. It was a typhoon, hurricane and tidal wave rolled into one. Even when I explained it was to help my overseas travel plans, Mother said she would not have a member of the family involved in such a common occupation as salesgirl, and she wasn't prepared to discuss the matter. That's where it ended. It was not discussed again, and here I am.'

'There would be pressures, recriminations,' Jancy said slowly. 'You haven't been too hasty? Another week or two, until the problem was resolved . . . '

Susan shook her head. 'I had to make the first move. It took some doing, I can tell you, but at least Quent was behind me.'

'And Michael?' Jancy asked with studied nonchalance.

'Oh, him.' Susan sniffed. 'Michael blows with the wind, I'm afraid. Whatever's best for Michael is best for everybody else. He'll get on, my big brother.'

Jancy smiled. 'And we'd better get on, too, and back to work.'

Sigrid was a marvellous asset, both as a salesgirl and a professional seamstress, and Susan would be a great help, too, given time to learn. But there was still a tremendous amount Jancy had to do personally, keeping the accounts, arranging window and model displays, designing new clothes for autumn and winter.

She had decided to spend part of her precious hoard of money on newspaper, television and radio advertising, and, while this was expensive, she hoped it would pay dividends sooner or later. Certainly trade was increasing daily and the extra volume of business presented further problems.

Besides, she had been dwelling too much on Michael of late. Since the telephone had been installed he had called her twice. He was always preoccupied with other matters, busy with running the Irongates property. So many reasons and excuses, all of them time-consuming and sending him off to distant places.

Still, she could afford to wait and let circumstances take their natural course. She was content with the small crumbs of affection he threw her, but, for the present, was determined to maintain her independence. So she accepted Arnie's invitation to go to a drive-in cinema in Canberra.

He called for her at six-thirty. The late afternoon sun was a ball of fire. All the way to the capital, on narrow roads that wound through brown-grassed pastures, through long avenues of gum trees forming canopies overhead, they talked about Jancy's progress in the garment business.

When they reached the drive-in cinema it was half-filled with cars. Arnulf parked near the projection booth and led Jancy through the rows of vehicles to the spacious, window-walled snack bar and concessionaires. Near by, a jumbo-sized barbecue was providing a constant supply of sizzling steaks, chops and sausages to hungry patrons making a night out of the film show.

Arnie found a vacant table in the adjacent dining area, with gaily-painted weatherproofed furniture, and pulled out a chair for her.

'Reserve the other chair for me and I'll be back soon with a couple of steaks. Rare, medium or well-done?'

'Well-done,' she answered. 'And with plenty of chips. I'm a great chip-eater, Mr Vigeland.'

'I'm just a great eater, Miss Talliman,' he quipped. 'Don't go away. I'll be keeping an eye on you.'

'Likewise, in case some other girl attracts your attention.'

Idly she watched him join the queue for the barbecued meals, amused and grateful for his flippancy. On that basis their relationship was that much simpler, that much more satisfying in its quiet, unemotional affections.

Then she gazed about her, already enjoying the evening immensely, at the giant screen showing slide advertisements, at the children's playground adjoining the dining area, with swings, see-saws and slippery-dips, and at the coming and going of the cool and casually dressed patrons.

Each and every one was a stranger, but she did not feel alone or alienated from them. For the moment she was relaxed in her own company, content to be a spectator on the noisy, energetic mainstream of life ebbing and flowing about her. Wrapped in silence, she gave herself voluntarily to the pleasure of the night.

It was the first time she had been to a drive-in cinema, and she found it lively and stimulating.

Children of all ages swept past the tables, hands grasping ice-cream cones and confectioneries. Young lovers sauntered hand-in-hand, parents shepherded their offspring from one youthful distraction to another.

The day was almost done, and red galleons sailed the turbulent clouds of the western sky. Another fine, hot day tomorrow, she thought. Sigrid said it would be. A fine and sunny, lots-of-passing-travellers day. The weather was drawing them in droves to the south coast beach resorts.

'Hello, Miss Talliman,' came a soft, familiar voice, and snapping out of her reverie Jancy glanced up sharply.

'Oh . . . Miss Meddow,' Jancy said with surprise. The heiress of the Peppertree property was accompanied by an older woman who carried a carton of soft drink in each hand.

'Mrs Franklin,' Cynthia went on, 'this is Jancy, of Jancy's Boutique, in Bungalan. Strange that we should meet here,' Cynthia added. 'We were talking about you, and the beautiful clothes you stock, less than an hour ago.'

The older, grey-haired woman's eyes sparkled with interest. 'I've seen your advertisements in the newspaper,' Mrs Franklin gushed. 'I believe you're doing very well indeed out at the village. A pity you're not in town here. You'd do even better in Canberra, I'm sure. Cynthia tells me you have a delightful range.'

Jancy gave Cynthia a nod of appreciation. 'That's very kind of her. Would you both like to sit down until my escort returns?'

'We have our own,' Mrs Franklin said. 'So sorry, I'd love to hear more of the boutique, but my husband is practically dying of thirst. He was too lazy to get out of the car.'

'Now that's unfair, Grace,' Cynthia chastised her gently. 'We wanted to stretch our legs, if you recall.' Then: 'Michael tells me Susan is working at the shop.'

Immediately on the defensive, Jancy paused for the right words: 'I needed assistance and offered her the job. She's quick to learn and dotes on the boutique atmosphere.'

'I gather the current sixty-four-dollar question is whether her mother is enjoying or doting on it,' Cynthia said with wry amusement. 'Mrs Rickwood, I hear, is rather upset about it.'

Jancy shrugged. 'Susan is free to give notice whenever she chooses. I assure you there was no intent to cause family discord — though I am well aware Mrs Rickwood considers the rag trade a, shall we say, lowly occupation.'

Cynthia stared at her speculatively for a few moments. 'I thoroughly approve of Susan's move,' she said quietly. 'She's never been a happy girl, always chafing at the bit, resenting her lack of choice and freedom. She has to learn for herself it's a great big world beyond the boundaries of Irongates. She desperately needs company and other interests.'

'That's true,' Jancy agreed. 'Also important is the fact that Susan has been working for three days, since Monday, and her mother has not raised any objections, at least not to me.'

'Nor is she likely to,' Cynthia said. 'She'll raise them in more devious ways. Don't get me wrong. There is a lot to admire in Helena Rickwood. She is a remarkable countrywoman, outstanding in property management. But as a mother, she wears a velvet glove on an iron hand.' Cynthia laughed softly. 'Don't tell her I said so.'

To Jancy the trend of the conversation was frankly astonishing. She had presumed, erroneously so it appeared, that Michael's coiffured and elegant old dragon and Cynthia Meddow, of the Peppertree Meddows, were as thick as the proverbial thieves.

Joining the group at a most opportune time, Arnie Vigeland slid two cardboard plates on to the picnic-style table.

'Good evening, ladies,' he said cheerfully.

Jancy made the formal introductions. 'Arnie is a friend of mine. He was the chief foreman on the repairs and decorations job at the boutique. I could never have managed without him or his mates.'

'Anytime you have a day to spare,' Mrs Franklin said, 'my sunroom is in need of a magic wand. I could do with a painter, a strong man about the house. Peppertree is perfect as it is, so I guess all Cynthia wants is the strong man. A pity she didn't bring him along tonight.'

Cynthia did not speak. She and Arnulf Vigeland were looking at each other, Arnie with the endearing lop-sided grin on his chunky face, and Cynthia wide-eyed and inscrutable.

Grace Franklin chattered on. The words emerged in a torrent, spilling on deaf ears. Slowly, Jancy pushed back her chair and got to her feet.

The air was charged with a human electricity as two self-assured, self-contained personalities confronted each other in wary challenge. Jancy felt the current turned on, felt it crackling, flowing between them, man to woman, woman to man. She felt the buttressed impact as their individual auras collided and dissolved into something private, secretive, all-consuming.

The thickset, virile and stocky work-man and the self-possessed squatter's daughter.

The same kind of invisible chemistry that had once united Jancy and Michael, though the reaction had been more gradual. The same emotional forging that could build a towering monolith to love, or wreck several lives in its foundations of abandoned passion.

It wasn't happening, it couldn't happen — such instant attraction, such immediate physical awareness. But Jancy knew it had.

5

A month had passed and the summer heat had grown less intense. With March turned into mellowing April, the days were milder and infinitely more bearable.

For Jancy Talliman, however, the pleasant days were crammed and hectic. The passage of five frenetic weeks, filled day and night with a multitude of business activities and decisions, had barely given her time to breathe, let alone savour the welcome change in climate.

Not that she would have had it otherwise, since the same activities prevented her, in part, from dwelling too much on Michael Rickwood and their relationship.

Unsatisfactory was a mild description for the romance, if the boy-loves-girl word, with its tender interpretations, was applicable.

No, it would hardly qualify as a

romance. It was more an attachment, an involvement, an association of the sexes. She was simply a side in an emotional triangle. Or a square, if Helena Rickwood were included in the human geometry.

Many a dark and lonely evening, isolated from the community in her upstairs flat and concentrating on the paperwork demanded in the efficient running of the business, Jancy would pause to consider and to fret.

Michael had been to visit Jancy twice since the gala opening of the boutique, on both occasions discreetly after dark. Once they had had dinner together, the second time they had shared each other's company until two o'clock in the morning, talking the hours away.

With his car parked in the street outside at that gossipy time of night, or early morning, it was a wonder everybody in the village and the district wasn't pairing them off as lovers advertising the affair.

But, curiously, their private meetings

had not become common property. The several times they had been together, in a couple of months, were scarcely enough to set the world on fire.

Very early in the piece she had summed up the situation, and kept on summing it up for reassurance. If Michael was involved with Cynthia, he would have to extricate himself as best he could. Unless he was playing a selfish game of his own, enjoying the favours of both contenders while he reviewed the assets of his future. There was no doubt whatever in Jancy's mind he was an ambitious, even ruthless, man who knew exactly what he wanted and where and how to get it.

And, because she had the shop and its commitments and was likewise ambitious, though on a different tangent, Jancy had long decided to play it cool, to accept Michael at face value. It was difficult, of course, and destructive, and though she tried desperately not to cling to or possess him, she often feared for her own happiness if she showed jealousy and disinterest or if she sent him away.

So, accepting what life had to offer, for the moment, she was prepared to accept also the affection he gave her, on his terms, and wait for the complications to untangle themselves.

Arnulf Vigeland was helping there. Sigrid knew a little, but not much. Arnie, Sigrid mentioned casually one morning, had taken a girl to dinner at a Canberra nightclub. And another time, she went on, relishing the snippets of information concerning her brother, Arnie had gone on a Sunday picnic across to the south coast.

'Who's the lucky companion?' Jancy had asked, offhand.

Sigrid hadn't known the girl's identity, but, adding two and two together, something was in the wind. Arnie, she said, had developed a crush on someone.

Wednesday morning was rather slack and, with Susan and Sigrid to cope with any individual customers who might call in, Jancy strolled along the wide main street of Bungalan to the post office.

She was a familiar figure now in the village, and every few yards a child, a storekeeper or a passing resident gave her a smile or a cheerful greeting.

Jancy had written several letters to Melbourne. After weeks of procrastination she had finally decided to spend several days in the Victorian capital, to call on dress manufacturers and wholesale warehouses dealing in handbags, accessories and other items she carried in stock.

So she had written to these people, also to a city hotel for accommodation, and proposed to fly down from Canberra in about a fortnight.

The post office was situated about half a block up from the Anglican church, a sandstone colonial edifice fenced with towering pines.

Mrs Freda Mason was seated behind the post office counter, her grey-haired head lowered over her lap as she worked on a piece of material with needle and thread.

As Jancy banged the fly-wire door, Mrs Mason glanced up.

'Having a bit of a break?' the elderly woman asked pleasantly. The widowed postmistress was in her mid-fifties, a tall and angular woman who had lived most of her life in Bungalan.

'I needed the walk and the fresh air,' Jancy said, and asked for stamps.

'You seem to be very tied up in the business,' the postmistress continued affably. 'All work and no play . . . '

Jancy laughed. 'Makes me a very dull girl. I know. That's just how I feel. I expect I am rather dull, once away from the boutique.'

Mrs Mason had been in the shop twice since it opened, to buy a cheaper-priced dress and a pair of gloves for Sunday church service.

'Have you worn that striped shirt-maker I sold you?' Jancy asked conversationally.

Mrs Mason nodded. 'Once. To a

meeting of the ladies' guild. The dress suits me; I feel comfortable in it.'

Jancy smiled. 'That's the important thing, to feel the good fit of a garment. It really suited you.'

Then she noticed the item the postmistress had been sewing; a brown collar for a dress, and half of it exquisitely embroidered with seed pearls and clear glass beads.

'How lovely,' Jancy said, pointing to the collar. 'You do embroidery, I see.'

The woman seemed overcome with modesty. 'It's my speciality, Miss Talliman. It takes patience more than anything else, and I have lots of that. With so few customers here, if I didn't find something else to do I think I'd go balmy.'

Suddenly Jancy remembered Miss Henley, a wealthy Canberra spinster, who wanted Jancy to design her an evening dress for a charity function in Sydney. Beads and pearls, Jancy mused. Miss Henley was certainly the type, and had chosen an oyster-grey silk with floating panels. With her slim build the middle-aged spinster would carry it beautifully, having a splendid figure for her age.

'Would you consider doing some embroidery for me?' Jancy asked. 'As a paid job, of course. I have a special customer . . . '

Mrs Mason's eyes lit up with pleasure. 'Of course I would. I'd love to. And I'm fairly fast. Yes, I'd really like that very much.'

Jancy licked several stamps and attached them to her mail.

'Fine. I'll let you know as soon as the final design I'm working on is approved. The customer wants an original creation.'

'You must be kept very busy at the boutique,' Mrs Mason went on. 'The shop . . . it's the talk of the village, you know. A bit of new blood in the place was badly needed. And everybody is profiting. Mr Fowler of the Empire is selling more beer than ever before, what with all the husbands filling in time while waiting for their wives. Peter told me that.'

'Peter?' Jancy queried, enjoying the little chat in the post office.

'A nephew. Peter Mason. My brother-in-law's eldest boy. He's a proper Jack-of-all-trades.'

'That's a handy bit of news to store away,' Jancy said reflectively. 'A good tradesman is hard to find in these parts.'

Mrs Mason nodded agreement. 'That's perfectly true. But Peter needs work and his charges are reasonable. He used to be employed in Sydney, but didn't like the rush and bustle. He's always been a country lad at heart. Though I must admit,' and Mrs Mason gave a hearty chuckle, 'he's hardly a boy. Six feet tall and twenty-two years of age.'

Jancy said cautiously: 'Maybe, if he has a few minutes to spare sometime, he could call into the shop. I have certain ideas about the upstairs flat. It's so old-fashioned and depressing. If I could have it tidied up a bit, made to

look more comfortable and attractive . . . '
She couldn't possibly allow the men at
the dam to organise another working
bee.

'Oh, he could do that all right,' the
postmistress assured her. 'And his
quotes are without obligation.'

*   *   *

To Jancy's surprise the young man called
the same day, in the cool of the evening.

Immediately Jancy summed him up
as a nice lad, if he could be considered
a lad at such a manly age. Tall and
beanpole thin, he had long, thick titian
hair in need of a trim, and strong, white
teeth that could have graced any
toothpaste advertisement.

'What's the problem, Miss?' was his
opening remark at the front door.

'Come on in,' Jancy greeted, amused
and pleased by his promptness. 'I'll explain
as we go along. I didn't expect you so
quickly.'

'My aunt — Mrs Mason — sent a

message home. If you want a job done and decide I'm to do it, then let's get cracking. I need the wages.'

Jancy laughed at his blunt approach. 'You're a fast worker, I can see.'

'Not all that fast. Reliable.'

Jancy's eyebrows lifted. 'Well, I've heard that personal recommendation is the best kind.'

Sigrid was having a salad tea with Jancy, prior to returning to her own accommodation at the hotel. When Peter Mason walked in she had finished her meal and was stacking the dishes in the sink.

'Meet Sigrid Vigeland,' Jancy said. 'She helps me in the boutique. Sigrid, this is Peter Mason, who will probably be gilding the lily with a paintbrush and wallpaper trough.'

Peter looked at the Norwegian girl with interest. 'I've seen you about from time to time.' And flashed his beautiful teeth. In half an hour he had prepared an estimate for painting and paperhanging.

When the young man had gone and

Sigrid was washing the dishes preparatory to leaving also, the girl asked: 'Were you happy with the price quoted, Jancy? He seems honest enough.'

Jancy was drying a dinner plate. 'I've practically decided to accept it. But not this side of the buying trip to Melbourne. I can't delay that too much longer to order spring stocks.'

'In other words, you expect to be here at that time of year and the shop is going well.'

Jancy smiled at her astuteness. 'The accountant in Canberra thinks we'll have a goldmine, given time, patience and energy. Yes, as you're no doubt aware, business is improving week by week.'

'I rather thought it was,' Sigrid said candidly. 'Of course, being out the back most of the time, I can't count the customers. I'm so glad. I wouldn't ever want to go back to slaving for Mr Fowler.'

★　★　★

It had been a hectic Saturday morning, with sales and profits soaring from the special busload of shoppers brought out from Canberra and the neighbouring town of Queanbeyan.

The idea was Susan's, who had solicited Quentin's flair for organisation.

'If a special bus was chartered for, say, forty women for half a day, what might the hiring charge amount to?' Susan had mused when she and Quentin were at home watching television one evening. Quentin knew so many people, in so many occupations.

Her brother made a rough mental calculation.

'Of course,' he began, before committing himself, 'a lot depends on the mileage covered. That's a consideration. And the hours the bus driver remains on duty.'

Susan was figuring her own mathematics. 'If it cost one dollar twenty per head and each woman spent, say, sixteen or twenty dollars, Jancy would still be in front, and gain a percentage of new customers.'

In his deep leather armchair Quentin clasped his hands behind his curly-haired head.

'That's sound reasoning. If you want to go from there with facts and figures, I know a bloke who could fix you up with a one-price deal.'

'Not me,' Susan corrected. 'Jancy Talliman.'

'And what's your commission, Miss Big Business?'

Susan waved aside such mercenary details. 'Oh, I'm not expecting to profit from it. I thought it up out of friendship.'

Quentin grinned. 'From my experience, friendship and business don't mix.'

Jancy had been delighted with the scheme, especially since she had accomplished all she had set herself to do in Melbourne. Also there had been the pleasure of the unexpected.

It was now the end of April and winter garments she had ordered from manufacturers earlier in the year were already starting to come through by interstate and intrastate carriers.

As well she had designed a large number of outfits herself for special customers, and Sigrid had been busy making them up.

'If it pays off,' Jancy said to Susan, 'perhaps we could continue the bus charter on a regular basis, possibly the first Saturday of each month.' She smiled. 'Time enough to give the girls a chance to save for the next big spending spree.'

Though more in control of her emotions, Jancy was as enthusiastic as her employee about the idea.

Quentin's friend arranged the hire of the bus. Jancy included the proposed bus trip to Bungalan in her normal advertising, and all seat tickets were sold within a week.

The venture was an outstanding success. The boutique was crowded to overflowing, and it was busier than on the shop's opening day, months previously. The women, of all ages, young and not so young, enjoyed the atmosphere of the shopping excursion and Jancy contributed further to this by borrowing crockery and glasses from Samuel Fowler — at a nominal charge — and serving sherries and coffee, with biscuits and cream cake supplied by the bakery.

So, for all concerned, it developed into a happy and satisfying morning. The bus travellers bought well and, in several instances, recklessly. By eleven o'clock, with coast road travellers waiting to be attended to, women from Warabee and the coach passengers having the time of their lives, Jancy sent an SOS to Mrs Mason for another pair of hands. There was no one else she could think of or consider dependable, on the spur of the moment.

As the post office closed at eleven and the widow was available, she came immediately, quite delighted by Jancy's need for village help.

By one o'clock, well past the normal

closing time, the customers were reluctantly eased out. Jancy insisted upon paying Mrs Mason for her troubles and, as appreciation for the extra business, Susan was given a ten-dollar bill tucked into an envelope.

An hour later her assistants had gone for the weekend, Susan off to visit a friend who lived on a dairy farm in the flat pastures along the Warabee dam road, and Sigrid accepting an invitation from Peter Mason to go horse-riding.

So now she was alone, weary but well pleased with the morning's effort.

When the knock sounded on the front door of the shop she was straightening up as best she could the aftermath of the morning's onslaught of trading.

Frowning at the interruption, she opened up, prepared to kindly but firmly tell whoever the caller was that the boutique was closed until the Monday morning.

The last person she expected to find standing there on the footpath was

Helena Rickwood. To Jancy's disadvantage, the total astonishment registered instantly and for a moment her mind went blank from the shock of the confrontation.

Perceiving the reaction, Michael's mother immediately pursued the initiative.

'Since the shop is not open for business, I'm not here to buy,' she said crisply. 'I came primarily to have a talk with you.'

She may have had the opening initiative, but Jancy soon realised she had an advantage also, of being on her own ground, on home territory. For a few brief moments she was almost tempted to reject the request for a 'talk', to curtly refuse without so much as an explanation for her refusal.

But it was apparent that Helena Rickwood had deliberately chosen this time of day, when Jancy was sure to be on her own on the premises, and without the possibility of interruption or third person intrusion into a personal and private conversation.

Jancy brushed a sweep of honey-coloured hair back from her forehead, garnering precious moments for self-control and assessment of the situation.

'If you would care to come in, Mrs Rickwood . . . ' Then, deciding to be as gracious as the woman permitted: 'I'm about to brew a pot of tea. Would you care to join me?'

Mrs Rickwood looked at her steadfastly. 'That would be nice.'

Jancy led the way upstairs to the small dining-kitchen area, where she gave a gesture of deprecation. 'I'm afraid this isn't as elegant or as comfortable as your lovely home, Mrs Rickwood, but I'm hoping to have it freshened up shortly to make it more habitable. I'm only the tenant . . . '

Helena Rickwood sat at the table, with the air of the grand matriarch, and drew off her gloves.

'I take it, then, you've settled in here, Miss Talliman?'

As she filled the kettle and with her

back to the visitor, Jancy replied: 'I expect so. The boutique is progressing very well.'

'As my friends tell me. Including Cynthia.'

Jancy turned to face her adversary. There was no question the woman was an adversary; Jancy had recognised that from their first meeting. And even here, in the upstairs flat, the older woman's demeanour was one of masked hostility.

Well, Jancy thought, preparing for the storm, whatever Mrs Rickwood had on her mind, she'd come out with it sooner or later.

The conversation continued with carefully guarded topics. Then, when the tea was poured and Jancy seated opposite the woman, Mrs Rickwood spoke her piece.

'I understand, Miss Talliman, you are acquainted with my son, Michael.'

Jancy nodded. 'That is so. Had you forgotten? We've known each other for some time; we met in England.'

Mrs Rickwood sipped her tea. 'I

understand also he has called here on several occasions.'

'Yes.' Jancy conceded that truth. 'There's been nothing secretive or immoral about it. We're ... good friends.'

'I can hardly believe that.'

Jancy gazed levelly at Michael's mother, at her immaculate hair, the clear eyes and hard mouth that even cosmetics could not soften, at the expensive string of pearls about her throat.

'Mrs Rickwood,' Jancy began carefully, setting down her teacup because her hand was trembling from suppressed anger. 'You are perfectly aware that Michael and I met while he was abroad. We were ... very good friends. But not lovers, if that's the question troubling you. We parted, and he came home. Naturally, living in the same district, we have met again, several times, on the same relationship.'

Which was untrue, so far as it concerned Jancy. The relationship was not the same, but markedly different. It had deteriorated and, somehow, was continuing to deteriorate.

'Then a fact of which you must be well aware, Miss Talliman, is that Michael is engaged to Cynthia Meddow. His visits here are causing an awkward if not unpleasant situation for . . .'

Interrupting her, Jancy said quickly but firmly: 'Michael assures me he is not engaged, and certainly Miss Meddow does not wear a ring to signify Michael's intent of marriage.'

Mrs Rickwood shrugged. 'A ring is merely a piece of jewellery. Many young people become engaged without one. In this day and age it scarcely has the same . . .'

'Ring or not,' Jancy went on, 'Michael told me himself he is not officially engaged.'

'He is unofficially engaged,' Helena Rickwood insisted. 'And his association with you is provoking a great deal of embarrassing comment. This is a small community, and people talk. Michael has known dear Cynthia since childhood. They have always been close and deeply attached . . . Surely you must realise a wedding is inevitable. They enjoy the same things and have common interests.'

With a flush, Jancy retorted: 'I've no doubt of that. Irongates and Peppertree, for instance.'

Mrs Rickwood's eyes slanted and grew dark. 'That too, since you mention it. It's a perfect union of the spiritual and the material. Country people whose roots are in the earth, whose ancestors, descendants, came here to open up the land . . . We're a different breed in the Bungalan district, Miss Talliman.'

'Yes, I've noticed the difference,' Jancy said drily. 'However, I cannot accept your statement that Michael proposes to marry Miss Meddow.'

Helena Rickwood tensed and straightened herself against the wood-backed chair. 'You want my son for yourself?' she demanded.

The question was so blunt, so outrageously indecent, that Jancy flinched. Did she want Michael for herself? She had pondered on that possibility a hundred times, without reaching a positive answer. Her mind concluded one thing, her heart another. Love was a devious torture.

Slowly she took the spoon from the saucer and stirred her tea. She had to do something physical; she had to think.

'I'm not sure,' she countered with a sigh, 'whether Michael wants me.'

'And if he does, even to the extent of deeply wounding his fiancée?'

Mrs Rickwood was over-dramatising the situation. Besides, Arnie Vigeland had entered the picture now.

'I don't know,' Jancy said, shaking her head in despair. 'I simply don't know.'

Mrs Rickwood toyed with her pearls. 'He may want you as a plaything, Miss Talliman, but you don't really understand Michael as I do, as his brother and sister understand him. You'll amuse the man for a while, that's undeniable, but he's ambitious, and selfish, and headstrong. And he's as much concerned about the future as he is with the present. For now I'm sure he enjoys dallying, a conquest here and there. Don't make the fatal mistake of thinking you're the only other girl who has afforded him diversion and temporary amusement. As for the future . . . he is well aware that Peppertree and its thousands of acres of valuable property could belong to him and his one day, by virtue of marital ties.'

Jancy took a deep, steadying breath. She didn't want to hear another word. 'Is that all, Mrs Rickwood?'

'Not quite all,' the older woman replied, with a mirthless smile as she started to draw on her gloves. 'As much as I want this wedding — and, being a mother, I confess to that — I will not tolerate Michael conducting a sleazy affair with you.'

'How dare you,' Jancy said, her head

starting to throb.

Imperiously, Mrs Rickwood held up a hand. 'One final thing. The last straw, the reason for me being here today, is that my elder son had the nerve, the temerity, to indulge in a clandestine meeting with you in Melbourne.'

Jancy felt nerves fluttering about inside her. 'It was not a clandestine meeting,' she corrected harshly. She had lost the verbal battle, but weeping — and she was close to that — would only add to the triumph of the victor. 'I had no notion Michael was in Melbourne when I flew down there.'

'He went to the wool sales, Miss Talliman. At least, he purported to have gone to them. I presume he did spend part of the time there, doing the job he was expected to do for Irongates.'

Jancy said: 'What Michael did with his time was his own affair. I spent mine with fashion manufacturers and dress material wholesalers.'

'But he did go to your hotel,' Mrs Rickwood probed sharply.

Jancy nodded. Yes, Michael had visited her hotel room. On her first night in the Victorian capital city she had been preparing for bed, worn out after the hectic rounds of a dozen business houses and appointments. It was hardly nine o'clock, but she had eaten and bathed and was very tired.

When she had seen Michael in the doorway, wearing his most endearing smile and carrying a bouquet of fresh flowers, she had almost burst into tears.

He had phoned room service and ordered drinks, and they had sat together, his arms about her, and talked until midnight. Then he had left, and she had not seen him since.

'Yes, he came to my hotel.'

'A very old and reliable friend of mine happened to be staying at the same hotel. She saw Michael going up in the lift — to your room.'

'And got in touch with you immediately, no doubt.' Jancy stood up, determined to end this farcical conversation. It had gone on long enough, beyond endurance. 'I can only assure you, Mrs Rickwood — and whether you believe me or not is irrelevant — it was not a prearranged, clandestine meeting. We behaved with absolute decorum. I say that only because you are Michael's mother; my personal affairs concern no one else.'

Helena Rickwood stood up also. 'You are quite wrong there, Miss Talliman. They concern many people. You have turned my daughter Susan into a rebel, you have caused a division between my son and the lovely girl he intends to wed. Indeed, with guile and interference, you seem to have taken over the entire village.'

Jancy faced her visitor, feeling a chill spread through her body.

Trembling with fury, she said: 'I don't wish to hear any more. I have lot of things to do, Mrs Rickwood. The shop demands my full attention.'

Helena Rickwood showed her teeth in a grimace meant for a smile. 'How fortunate you are,' she concluded, 'to even have a shop. To cater for such a mundane thing as the rag trade. I presume everything is in order with it?'

Jancy did not answer. Was that a threat, an implication that Mrs Rickwood was aware of something out of order? The lease with Samuel Fowler, the condition of the property itself?

Biting her lower lip, she led the way down the stairs and through the interior of the boutique, the older woman trailing behind.

Pulling the front door wide open, Jancy said, sardonically: 'Do call again, Mrs Rickwood.'

The mistress of Irongates swept past her on to the pavement outside. She turned: 'I very much doubt that, Miss Talliman. It is possible the premises could be closed, so I would have nothing to call at. Good-day.'

Jancy did not wait to see the woman get into her car. Slamming the door shut, she leaned against it, her heart thudding violently, her face chalk-white.

So it was a threat, by a powerful, rich and ruthless landowner. Jancy gazed down the length of the boutique.

What would Aunt Edith do or advise, she thought bleakly, tears brimming in her eyes. Oh, if only the dear old lady was with her still, offering comfort and encouragement, soothing away her fears and trepidations.

But that was wishful thinking. The dead remain buried and at peace.

But Aunt Edith had left her an important legacy, the strengths of determination and the discipline for self-survival. Nobody was going to undermine her business or take it away from her.

6

The year of the sparrows was approaching its zenith. Summer had lost its sting. With autumn in the air, crisping the nights and early mornings, poplar and maple trees were turning to gold.

Jancy had shampooed her hair and was brushing it, seated at the bedroom window and idly looking out across the main street and over the rusted rooftops opposite, to the plains of Bungalan.

Sparrows scurried and scampered in the guttering overhead, pecking along the metal trough and bickering in noisy chirps among themselves. The birds were perched in a string on the telegraph wires above the bakery, and a family of them had congregated on the nearest pole. So many little brown sparrows. There seemed to be more birds about than villagers.

What was it Quentin had told her all

those long weeks ago? A sparrow year was a year of fortune, of seasonal plenty. Something to that effect.

Jancy gave a wry smile at such superstitious nonsense. Good fortune? Plenty? Perhaps.

A week had elapsed since Helena Rickwood had called on her in such a peremptory manner, a week of fretful worry.

Susan had not come in to work on the Monday. Sounding tearful, she had phoned about ten in the morning to say she wasn't well. Jancy had not made an issue of it. Accepting the vague excuse and convinced Susan's mother was behind the girl's absence, Jancy told her to take care of herself and to return to the shop when she felt better.

All through the day she nursed that problem, too. Had there been a blow-up at the Rickwood homestead over Susan's employment? Had Mrs Rickwood finally wielded total authority over the girl? Had Susan capitulated?

With thoughts similar to Jancy's,

Sigrid also was upset, but by tacit agreement they did not discuss Susan or the state of her health. After the confrontation in the flat above the shop, Jancy was expecting anything to happen. But after Susan's phone call she realised that if the girl did not come back to the shop within a reasonable time, she would have to find a suitable replacement.

To their relief and surprise, Susan appeared on the doorstep ready for work at nine the following morning. Her pretty face was pale and drawn, but she offered no further information on the medical cause of her day off.

In the circumstances, Jancy decided, it was wiser to leave well alone. Sooner or later, Susan might confide in her. And if not, the family dispute would remain a private matter.

She had finished brushing and drying her hair when the telephone rang, and she hurried downstairs to answer it.

'Hello, there,' came Quentin's cheerful voice. She hadn't heard from him in ages. 'What do you have planned for this glorious Sunday? Care to elope?'

'Not without a month's notice,' she laughed, pleased he had bothered to call. 'What do you have planned?'

'A picnic. You bring the eats and I'll provide the transport and a jug of wine.'

'Anywhere special, Quentin?'

'On the river bank, in the south-west corner of Irongates. A beautiful spot, and secluded. Weeping willows, lush green grass and enough depth of water for a swim. So bring your bikini.'

A picnic on the family property? Quentin couldn't possibly be serious.

She said slowly, a firmness creeping into her voice: 'I'm afraid . . . is that the best place you can think of? If it is, then I'd rather not.'

'Don't be silly,' he chided. 'There's nothing awkward or difficult about the situation. It's miles from the homestead. You're not scared of my old mum, surely.' His teasing did not amuse her.

'Now you're being silly,' Jancy retorted, her feelings ruffled.

'Well then, what's the problem? You've not had a decent tour of Irongates and I'd like to remedy that.'

'I think the point is relatively unimportant, Quentin.'

'Not in brother Michael's book. Irongates is the stuff of fortunes, of colonial history and all that jazz.'

'Your history, maybe. His fortune. Certainly not mine.'

There was a pause on the other end of the line. Then Quentin went on, in a change of mood: 'You're being stuffy. English stuffy. Remind me to buy you a bottle of castor oil. That's a remedy of another kind.'

Tersely she asked: 'Are you trying to needle me?'

His laugh was hollow. 'Why should I bother? You've been needling yourself as long as I've known you. Anyway, let's stop quibbling. The dragon lady has gone to Queanbeyan for the day — one of her charitable causes — and Susan's doing some housework. Not before time, either. So how about it?'

Was his omission of reference to Michael's whereabouts deliberate? He came and went so often, flying here and there, from State to State. Were the frequent trips necessary? And why did Michael get all the plums? Why didn't Quentin go occasionally, to share in the trips away from routine labours on the property? These thoughts flashed through Jancy's mind as she contemplated a suitably framed answer.

'Okay, okay,' Quentin said, almost churlishly. 'I withdraw the offer. We'll skip the picnic. See you in church.'

'Wait!' Jancy cried spontaneously, but she was too late. Quentin had already cradled the receiver and the line was dead.

She felt wretched. To have been so petty, almost spiteful, to such a good friend. That kind of treatment had been unworthy of her, and unfair to him.

For a few miserable moments Jancy stood by the telephone, ashamed, and wishing they were face to face so that he could see she was troubled and eager to apologise for such beastly behaviour. She wasn't normally so churlish, ungracious. But reasons or excuses for the ill-humour could not repair the damage she had caused.

Would he phone again? He might; he was not the type of man who took offence easily. But when ten minutes passed and the phone did not ring again, she took the initiative.

Quentin answered and was polite but distant.

'I'm sorry,' Jancy said in a rush. 'I was feeling morose, out of sorts. I'm all right now. If the invitation still holds, I'd love to go on a picnic to the river.'

His tone was hesitant. 'You're quite sure?'

'I'm positive. Please forgive me. Besides,' she added, flattering him, 'you're bright company, Quentin. Maybe some of the brightness will rub off on me.'

'Thanks for the plug,' he said, scarcely taken in by her compliment.

'I'll pick you up about eleven o'clock.'

He arrived at a quarter past the hour, the Land-Rover screeching to a halt outside the shop. She had packed a small cardboard carton with food and filled a thermos with coffee and was ready to leave immediately.

As she slipped into the seat beside him Jancy said chattily: 'I brought the bikini, as you suggested. It's certainly warm enough for a dip in the stream. Did you bring your bathing togs?'

'I'm wearing them,' he said, and drove off in a burn of rubber.

For the first few miles of the journey Jancy wondered if she had made a mistake. Quentin was not exactly cool or uncommunicative, but his normally laconic and easy-going attitudes were subdued. It was as if some secret burden was weighing heavily on his mind. Either that or he was still nursing the grievance of Jancy's attitude on the telephone.

If Jancy was to blame for his frame of mind, the least she could do was make amends and pretend she was unaware of the constraint.

So she talked inconsequentially about anything and everything, whatever came into her head, but taking care to avoid contentious issues.

She told him about Peter Mason's quote to freshen up the flat, about the new wallpaper she had bought for half-price at a sale in Melbourne, and about the day-by-day happenings, some amusing, at the boutique.

Gradually, as she chattered on, Quentin began to unwind and relax. Perhaps it was the fine autumn day, ablaze with warm sunshine, or maybe simply a change of heart, but before long he was almost his old self. Almost, but not quite. He was still a little on guard, a trifle aloof and formal.

Finally, as the Land-Rover bumped over the cattle grid between the brick pillars leading to Irongates, Jancy said, throwing discretion aside: 'Are you still annoyed with me, Quentin? Look, I've worked like crazy to make amends, but if you're regretting the invitation, let's call it off right now before we drive any farther.'

She paused, starting to feel depressed. 'I behaved badly, I admit, and wish I hadn't. So I'm trying to make amends for the inexcusable manners.'

'They were pretty bad,' he conceded, 'but not inexcusable. You're changed, Jancy.'

She looked straight ahead, along the gravel road they were traversing. This was a different side to Quentin, one she had not been aware of previously.

'For better or worse, Quentin?'

'A bit of both, I guess. Better in business, that's perfectly apparent . . . '

'And worse in . . . ?'

'Impatience. Testiness. Reaction to people. You're more on the defensive, more aggressive . . . '

'Well,' she said, mounting her high horse. 'That's good to hear. Thanks for the personal criticism. Turn around, Quentin, and kindly take me home.'

'There you go again, lashing out

. . . Where is your home?' he asked, ignoring the imperious command. 'Sometimes you give the impression of being an alien, a displaced person, not quite belonging here, no longer tied to England. Yes, you're not the girl you used to be, and that's for sure.'

For a while she did not answer. Tears misted her eyes and she blinked them savagely away. If she wasn't the girl she used to be, other people had changed, too. Michael, who professed to care for her but who remained tantalisingly out of reach; Mrs Rickwood, who had stepped up the cold war with the big guns of intimidation; and now Quentin. Today she was discovering other, discouraging facets of the man's character and personality.

Jancy turned from him. The proposed picnic had turned into a fiasco. 'Please take me back. There's no point in going on.'

'There's no point in going back,' he answered gently, and the innuendo was not lost to her. She lapsed into silence, her head lowered, her moist eyes fixed on her lap.

'That's what you've been doing, Miss Jancy Talliman. Going back — to England; Kensington, wasn't it? — to Michael.' The grin twisted his mouth. 'Don't tell me it's not my concern. It isn't, so why should I worry? But you're getting hurt in the process. You can never recall the past, and as the present is so temporary, all that's left is the future, to aim at, to work for, to build the stuff of dreams. Am I making sense? Are you getting the message?'

She nodded, still averting her face.

'Are you in love with him?'

'I don't know,' she said wretchedly. 'Does that make sense? I was once, madly in love, in the past. I think I still am, but the situation is getting out of hand. It's ridiculous. I'm a grown woman, I should know my own mind.'

Quentin shook his head, and changed down a gear for pot-holes on the track ahead.

'It's not easy, sorting out emotional entanglements. The more you try to reason them out, the more confusing they become. But invariably light shines through the darkness, and then you wonder what the fuss was all about.'

'Thank you for that.'

So he really did understand. She gave a wan smile and straightened her sagging shoulders. Dear Quentin. If she lost him as a friend, he would be irreplaceable.

They were well into the Rickwood property, and now Quentin switched off his formerly difficult mood to become official guide of Irongates.

It was larger than any private parcel of land she had ever been on before. On her first visit, all she had seen was the homestead. But there was much more to Irongates than a spacious country residence.

As they drove round in the Land-Rover, Quentin paused briefly at the stockyards, spray sheep dips, the irrigation system, windmills and a number of dams.

'We have to keep up to the mark with equipment and facilities,' Quentin told her. 'It's a mechanised world today and the grazier has to use every modern innovation to save labour costs.'

He took her into a long shearing shed, empty and swept clean, and into buildings that housed machinery and vehicles.

For the first time Jancy began to appreciate the extent of the property and the wealth of the soil. Twelve thousand acres of sheep land made a sizeable hole in the countryside. Add the acreage of Peppertree to that of Irongates, and the combined area would represent a monumental backyard for any homesteader.

It was bait enough for any ambitious man to nibble at, to set as his goal.

Finally, Quentin said: 'Well, I think that's enough for now. I'm hungry, so let's start our picnic.'

It was an isolated area, the south-west corner of the Rickwood property, but scenically attractive.

'What do you think of it?' Quentin asked with veiled pride as he drove the Land-Rover to within twenty feet of the river bank. The grass was thick and spongy underfoot, and Jancy kicked off her sandals to walk to the water's edge.

The land was flat, part of the great plains, but parallel to the river as it meandered across the countryside ran a natural fence of trees and shrubs, beautiful weeping willows that trailed their delicate branches into the stream itself and, on the higher banks, created secret places behind curtains of leaves.

There was serenity here, contentment, an awareness of the earth itself.

Behind her, Quentin said: 'Aren't you glad you came?'

She swung to him, her eyes shining. 'What a marvellous place. If it were mine I'd come here as often as possible, at every opportunity.'

'It's not always as calm. The river can be deceptive, wild and raging. It's flood country, you know. When I was a toddler I remember my father telling me about a flood that swept through Bungalan and wrought terrible havoc. The water took weeks to subside, and damage ran into millions of dollars, to property, to stock, to roads and bridges. Sheep by the hundred drowned or were swept away; cattle, too.'

Jancy tried to envisage the scene, but found it impossible. 'It looks so peaceful,' she said, hardly believing the river could change into such a destructive monster. Sunlight silvered the ripples and ruffles caused by the eddies of wind. 'And so inviting. I can't wait to have a swim.'

While Quentin got the picnic things out of the Land-Rover she strolled along the river bank and changed into her bikini behind a tree a hundred yards downstream. As she came back, carrying her skirt and blouse in one hand and underwear in the other, Quentin glanced up and gave an appreciative whistle.

'You look better than a movie star,' he grinned.

'Which movie star?' she wanted to know, pleased by the compliment.

'I could name a dozen.' He laughed merrily. 'Lassie, for one. You've been hiding your true light under a bushel, or a dress.'

Her figure was superb and her long, slim legs set off her body to perfection. Jancy had bought the floral-patterned bikini in Sydney before travelling to Bungalan and this was the first time an opportunity had presented itself for her to wear the two flimsy pieces of next to nothing.

'I'm beginning to understand,' Quentin added, taking off his shorts and shirt and standing there in a pair of Terylene racers in plain navy-blue, 'why other blokes have come a-courting . . .'

Jancy noted the broad shoulders, the tapered waist and the golden tan.

'You look pretty fit and athletic yourself. Since you mention it, why haven't girls come a-courting, to take you off the shelf?'

'Oh, they come all right.' He

shrugged. 'But I'm finicky. I've got ideas of my own.'

'Good luck, Quentin.'

'And good luck to you. And with those few words the mutual admiration society will go into recess. Hungry?'

'Yes, but I can wait half an hour longer.' She reached for a tablecloth and spread it over the grass. 'I'd like to lie here for a while and soak up the last of the summer sun.'

Quentin frowned. 'With that all-over English complexion, tinned peaches and cream, you wouldn't last twenty minutes. That sun's fierce today. You'd burn before being aware of it.'

'I'll take that risk, for fifteen minutes.'

'You won't,' he growled. 'Seems to me you take too many risks.'

He lay beside her on the substitute rug and she looked at him through narrowed eyes. 'What exactly was that crack supposed to imply?'

Quentin shrugged. 'The risk you've been taking with Michael. He's my brother; I've known him longer than you.'

She sat upright, sweeping long hair back from her forehead. 'Michael! Michael! Michael!' she burst out, her high horse rearing. 'Can't we forget that he exists, for a few hours at least?'

'Can you forget him?' Quentin asked lazily.

'For heaven's sake . . . ' What was the matter with Quentin? His chameleon moods were infuriating; riling her one moment, flattering her the next. 'From the moment you picked me up outside the shop this morning you've been spoiling for an argument. Well, I'm turning the other cheek. I refuse to quarrel with you. Anyway, I don't make candid observations about your amours.'

Quentin chewed on a blade of grass. 'That's because you don't know anything about them.'

'If I were curious enough . . . I could ask Susan.'

'She wouldn't have a clue. I never let

my left hand know what my right hand is doing.'

'One of those,' Jancy sniffed. 'I suggest you sit on them simultaneously and give them both a surprise.'

Quentin gave a loud hoot of laughter that sent several parakeets fluttering in alarm from the tallest boughs of a nearby gum tree. 'Say, that's funny. You have a sense of humour.'

'It wasn't meant to be funny,' Jancy retorted. 'It was meant to be sarcastic. You're not being funny, either.'

Quentin propped himself up on an elbow and gazed at her quizzically. 'You really are funny, but funny-peculiar. You're mixed up, confused. You need straightening out. If I wasn't a prospective brother-in-law I shouldn't fuss myself, or bother. However, since you admit to having designs on the family . . . '

Jancy balled her fingers into fists. 'Oh, Quentin,' she rebuked him wearily. 'I do appreciate all you've done for me in the past. But that doesn't give you the right to be snide, or contemptuous. Whatever are you talking about — designs on the family?'

Quentin gave her an exaggerated, confidential wink. 'The Rickwood inheritance.'

She swung away from him, too upset to answer. Why did he persist in antagonising her? Why did he keep harping so on his brother Michael and Jancy's association with him? If there was an ulterior motive behind his hurtful barbs, his changing attitudes, Jancy was unable to fathom them. The last thing she wanted was a falling out, a severance of their friendship. But he was provoking her, goading her towards it.

Determined to be pacifist, she said: 'All the picnic things are in the cardboard carton I brought. You prepare the luncheon.' She sprang to her feet. 'I'm going for a swim.'

'Wait!' he cried, reaching out a restraining hand. 'I'm coming with you.'

She did not want him with her. She needed a respite, a brief time for solitude, to compose herself, to mask her vulnerability. So she ran away from him, across the thick carpet of grass, to the river bank.

'Don't go in,' came Quentin's warning shout. 'It's not safe, only in certain places. Come back at once, you little fool.'

His warning fell on deaf ears. She weaved round the lacy, drooping branches of the willows, running parallel to the water until the bank fell away to a narrow beach, a strip of red sand that trailed the river for a hundred yards to its next gentle turning.

'You idiot,' Quentin roared, as he came sprinting after her. 'Stop, Jancy. Wait for me.'

The water caught the sun and was splashed with diamonds. She dived neatly and deeply, her eyes closed, the water cool and caressing as she speared into it.

Down and down she glided, revelling

in the pleasure of it, until her hands struck the slimed wood of a submerged tree. That brought her up sharply and telegraphed an instant danger signal. Arching her body, she twisted into an upright vertical position and kicked hard for the ascent to the surface.

Her bare feet registered the cold clamminess of decayed leaves and scratching branches, and then her right foot slipped through the leaves and her ankle was caught firm, held there twelve, fourteen feet in the depths of the river.

Jancy's heart raced and thudded in sudden panic. She opened her eyes, but the underwater was murky and vision restricted. Jack-knifing, she bent over the distorted shadows that were the boughs and foliage of the sunken tree, feeling along the trapped foot and jerking vainly in an effort to release it. But the more she tried to wrench it free, the more it became wedged in the tangle of branches.

She was running out of air and terror

was spreading through her like a malignant growth, gone berserk and beyond control. The heartbeats were tom-toms growing louder and louder in her ears, now pounding and reverberating as horror took possession. Her hands clawed at the water as she fought to reach the lifesaving air above.

Bubbles burst from her mouth and nose and her long hair floated about her face. Then the river became an abyss and she was sinking into it, down and down, falling lightly to her knees on the debris-covered tree and sinking into a fluid darkness of death.

Then, when all seemed lost, Quentin was there beside her, prising her foot loose, supporting her and carrying her up with him to the surface.

She fought her way slowly back to consciousness, gasping painfully and her vision impaired. All she could see was the picnic tablecloth, that too appearing to smother her. Quentin had straddled her waist and his hands were firm and strong as he worked on her lungs to empty them.

'Just lie there,' she heard him gasp. 'You'll be all right soon. Breathe slowly and try to regulate it. You're waterlogged.'

The tablecloth blurred. The ground heaved beneath her and the world began to spin. Her hands clutched at the grass to steady herself. Then she was released from the weight of him and her body was free again. She began to float, up and away.

'Quentin!' she called in distress and it came out a croak. She felt something soft being wrapped about her and she opened her eyes again and saw his white, strained face.

All at once she was terribly afraid. 'Hold me,' she sobbed, and kneeling beside her Quentin lifted her up and cradled her in his arms.

'I'm cold,' she wept. 'I'm so cold.'

'You're okay,' he soothed, stroking her wet and tangled hair. 'You probably feel awful, but it will pass, believe me.' Comforted and secure, she sank once more into oblivion.

7

Rain had fallen steadily for three days, and the countryside was drenched.

Of course, there would be lots of sunny days, Susan Rickwood had told Jancy, but it was a cold, flat part of the state, with fires blazing day and night, and oil heaters running non-stop.

She could hear the rain drumming on the corrugated-iron roof overhead and wondered, fleetingly, if there were leaks in the rusted iron, if the water would come through and damage the new paintwork and wallpapering Peter Mason had finished only two days before the weather changed.

He had done a splendid job, quite professional, and the upstairs flat, once so dingy and uninviting, was now much more cheerful.

She had simply discussed the job and left him to it, to pursue his decorating talents without interference. Not that she would have harassed him in the progress of his work. She had enough on her plate as it was.

Besides, she hadn't been feeling as well as she might. Half-drowned on the day of the picnic, she was still suffering from the effects of immersion in the depths of the river. To Quentin she owed her life. But since he had brought her home and got Sigrid, who had been available in her hotel room, to put the patient to bed and take over, she had not laid eyes on the man.

That was another nagging query in her mind, one of many plaguing her of late. She'd been too ill, too distraught, to thank him properly. For a fortnight she had been awaiting a suitable opportunity, meanwhile fretting over his prolonged absence. He could have phoned, appreciating her reluctance to ring him at Irongates; he could have dropped in for a chat, however briefly. But he had done neither.

Slowly, Jancy opened another carton

of winter clothing from the manufacturers, checking each garment against the invoices and hanging it on a nearby rack. Her actions were mechanical and she was making hard work of it, her thoughts elsewhere. Once or twice she found herself immobile, just standing there beside the large carton on the floor, a dress in her hands, as she stared unseeing into space. And once, for no sensible reason whatever, hot tears gathered and trickled down her face. What was happening to her? Everything was going wrong.

She felt utterly spent and depressed, not exactly ill and not exactly well; somewhere in between, listless, tense, over-tired and melancholy. She awakened tired and went to bed tired, and in between the days stretched out in hours and hours of dismal labour.

It was worse having to cover up, to wear a calm and composed front, to attend to the myriad details of the boutique, to talk with manufacturers' reps and make instant decisions on styles and prices, to pander to difficult but profitable customers, to give undivided attention when occasionally all she wanted to do was escape from everyone and everything, to run upstairs and slam the flat door behind her.

There had been other, allied problems as well. Sigrid had been off work with influenza the previous Friday and Saturday, and Arnie had collected her, wrapped in rugs and a topcoat, and whisked her back to the construction camp for Mrs Vigeland to take care of her ailing daughter.

And Susan was going about with a long face, burdened with family worries of her own. Mrs Rickwood, it appeared, had given her an ultimatum: resign from her menial job as a sales assistant or remove herself from the parental house.

'Would the dragon woman really throw you out?' Sigrid had asked, incredulous. Her own mother was soft and gentle and loving.

Disconsolate, Susan had shrugged, still the rebel but her courage waning. 'She's the iron in Irongates. And as tough as they come. I guess, if she wasn't built that way, we might never have survived the rough years after my father died. Mother was born and bred in the country and she knows all there is to know about running a property.'

Privately, Jancy had already come to terms with the fact that Susan's days at the boutique were numbered. She would be sorry to see the girl leave, yet secretly relieved. The battle of wills was too great a strain for the teenage girl; though resisting in futile combat she had lost the fight before it had begun.

With no help whatever from her brother Michael.

Michael! As she thought of the man Jancy paused, her face troubled. She was missing him more and more. He had only to phone and her firm intentions melted under the spell of his charms. The tones of his voice, the dominant personality that bridged the miles . . . What tenuous thread bound her to him?

A knocking sounded at the door and Jancy went to answer it. It could be Michael, come to cheer her up on this desolate day, or Quentin.

The caller was neither, but Mrs Vigeland who stood in the doorway wearing a smile of radiating pleasure.

'Jancy, dear,' she greeted, giving the surprised girl a warm, maternal hug. 'We have come to see you at last. Such weather, it creeps into the old bones, I can tell you.'

'We have both come.' From the side of the doorway, out of sight and playing games with her, Arnulf stepped into view. 'I hope you're delighted. What a day! Yes, I will have a drink, thank you, Jancy. Rum, if you have it.'

'Can we put the kettle on?' Mrs Vigeland asked, rubbing her hands together. 'We have been driving from the camp. Rain, rain, rain . . . all the way in. To bring Sigrid back to her room at the hotel.'

Jancy opened the door wider to admit her visitors. 'Of course, we'll have a cup of tea. And I have sherry, sweet or dry, so take your pick, Arnie.'

'What terrible hospitality,' Arnie grinned. 'I think I'd better drop into the pub later on. He'd give me a rum.'

'You mean he'd sell you one,' his mother laughed.

Quickly, Jancy made a pot of tea and poured half a tumbler of sherry for Arnie.

They were pleasant company and brightened her gloomy day considerably. The subjects they brought up for conversation were safe and inconsequential, and for the first time in ages Jancy found herself relaxed and at ease. Their simple affection accomplished that. They were lovely people, true friends, and her heart went out to them for their kindness.

An hour and three cups of tea later Selma Vigeland decided it was time to check on Sigrid.

'No need to rush back,' Arnie told his

mother. 'But when you get here we'll head for Warabee. It gets dark so quickly and the roads are in bad shape with so many storms. Pot-holes by the thousand.'

'The bad weather doesn't seem to be easing,' Jancy commented. 'You're being wise, Arnie.'

His half-smile was wry, deprecating. 'About some things, maybe. Not about others.'

'That makes two of us, birds of a feather,' Jancy said lightly.

'Ho, ho,' Arnie gave a mock laugh. 'I sense a secret there. Have you made some shattering error or blunder? Now's the time to confess, to get it off that beautiful chest of yours.'

Jancy began to clear the afternoon tea things. 'You're the one who should be confessing,' she countered, avoiding his questioning glance. 'I hear there's a strange woman in your life.'

Arnie chuckled boisterously and slapped his thigh in rough good humour. 'Any woman in my life is no stranger. Come on now, out with it. Whom do you have in mind? Someone special, I'm sure. She'd have to be special, to want to pick up with me. And close-lipped. I keep my love life pretty much under wraps.'

Jancy paused momentarily to reflect on the wisdom, or lack of it, in airing her knowledge, then plunged into indiscretion.

'Cynthia Meddow?'

'Ah!' Arnie wagged an admonishing finger at her. 'What secret service told you that?'

'It's a small village,' Jancy said. 'Unless you drive out into the backblocks to do your courting there's not much privacy.'

He helped her carry the dishes to the sink. 'Then I might as well admit it. I do drive into the backblocks and there is a woman in my life.'

'Do you see her often, considering the circumstances?'

'Not as often as I'd like. It's a queer set-up. There's this family thing between her and one of the Rickwood fellows; you know which one. There are internal pressures. Frankly, it's feudal. But this and that and the other add up collectively to a question of land. They're greedy, all right. I gather Cynthia's old man is as keen as the Rickwood old lady for a union of the clans. To stop the working class taking over, maybe.'

He was being facetious to cover up. Obviously, Cynthia had been frank and honest with him in that regard.

'The people at Peppertree are big wheels,' Jancy said, thinking that Cynthia was being more open with Arnulf than she was with Michael.

'Granted,' Arnie agreed, reaching for a tea towel. 'With due humility, I'm not such a small one myself.'

She half-smiled at his down-to-earth immodesty. 'It's not the big wheels or the little wheels,' she pointed out. 'It's the unity, the family wheels within wheels. If you get caught up in the cogs the Rickwood — Meddow machinery is liable to grind you into mincemeat.'

That was a risk he was prepared to take, Arnulf told her.

'Then you're really serious about Cynthia?'

'One day I will ask her to marry me.'

Jancy doubted if Michael ever would. Impulsively she turned and kissed him on the cheeks. 'She's a nice girl, a very nice person. And you're wonderful. I wish the pair of you every happiness.'

Arnie leaned back against the sink. 'Strange how things happen, how the road of life can take a different turning overnight. We never know what is round the bend. A month ago I hadn't a clue and then — wham! — there she is, available even with a few strings, and I'm a dead duck.'

'You're very much a live duck,' she corrected him. 'You know what you want along the road you mentioned and how best to get it. Not everyone is as fortunate.'

'You could be,' he said, a mischievous look on his craggy features. 'Of course, if I elope with Cynthia, then the field is left open for you.'

'What field?' Jancy asked, with disarming innocence.

'Michael Rickwood.'

So that relationship, too, was becoming public property. How many others knew?

Arnie went on: 'If we're playing a game of spilling the beans, let's be scrupulously honest with each other. With Cynthia swept off her feet and I'm sweeping very nicely, thank you, Mike's back in lone-wolf territory. So he's all yours, if you want him.' He gazed at her questioningly as she washed the dishes, the curl of his lips half-mocking. 'Do you really want him? You could do better.'

Jancy shrugged, a gesture that implied it was of small account. 'We all of us want things we can't have. It's human nature.'

Arnie nodded in agreement. 'And it's folly. But get yourself prepared, Jancy Talliman. You might get him on the bounce, and that's the easiest way of all, when he's vulnerable. Don't make the mistake of thinking he's your last hope. Half a dozen blokes back at the camp would marry you tomorrow, if they were game enough to propose.'

Jancy smiled, glad of the compliment but gladder still of the switch in the conversation. Scrupulous honesty was one thing; it could also be awkward and embarrassing. 'I appreciate the offers, and bear them in mind.'

Arnie said goodbye outside the boutique and from the shelter of the awning she waved him off. With Cynthia foremost in mind, he had no time for unnecessary or delaying pleasantries.

The man's crazy in love, Jancy thought with amusement as she watched the car speeding into the murky night. And envied him.

As she turned to enter, she noticed the message stickytaped to the door. The note was from Samuel Fowler, asking her to call in and see him when the time was convenient.

For a few moments she hesitated, wondering what the hotel-keeper had in mind. An increase in rental, probably. But since it was early in the evening, she decided to get the matter over and done with. A showdown was inevitable and the sooner it was settled the better.

Samuel Fowler was absent from the hotel. He had stepped out for a spell, the lanky barman told her, as he pulled beer on tap for half a dozen male drinkers in the bar. They had nothing better to do this desolate night than enjoy a few drinks and play a friendly game of darts.

Jancy preferred not to remain in the bar, with its male patrons. Through a doorway she caught sight of a blazing log fire, so hurried into the adjoining parlour to thaw out.

The crackle of wood and the leaping flames in the huge fireplace were so comforting and diverting she was not aware immediately of the other occupant of the room, seated out of draughts in the corner near the door.

Standing in front of the fire and pulling off her woollen beanie and gloves, she was enjoying the warmth provided by the management when a voice addressed her.

'A fine night for ducks, Jancy.'

She would have known that voice in any place at any time and, with recognition, her heart gave a peculiar lurch.

'Oh, it's you, Quentin,' she replied, composing herself before turning to him. 'What are you doing there, so far from the fire?'

'I'm quite warm enough here. I don't like being toasted. And I have to brave the weather again, sooner or later.'

His thick, unkempt dark hair was damp and raincurled. He sat at a table by the wall, with his chair pushed back and one long leg crossed over the other.

'You seem,' she said quietly, 'well satisfied with your own company tonight. Would you — be wanting mine?'

Better to get that problem straightened out, from the beginning.

'Take a pew,' he answered with a grand gesture to the chair beside him. 'It's a free country, with free seating in a free parlour. What have you been doing with yourself lately?'

His humour was not particularly amusing. 'Working hard, Quentin. As usual.' He had changed, in manner towards her, in tone of voice. She was convinced of that because she had sought for changes. He was more formal, slightly diffident, his demeanour coolly offhand.

How was this possible, she wondered, fretting already. They had been such good friends. And he had saved her life. She would always owe him that, even if their friendship foundered, even if she found herself rejected. But . . . why? What had brought about this drift in their formerly happy relationship? Was it Michael? No other simple or logical reason came to mind.

She crossed to Quentin, weaving

between the vacant chair and tables, and sat opposite him.

'I was almost sure — that is, I was hoping . . . you might have called into the boutique. That day of the picnic . . . it didn't end properly. I almost drowned in the river. I had it all worked out. You'd visit to see how I was and I would thank you.'

His blue eyes were less intense as though he had contrived to draw a veil across them and prevent others from peering into those windows of the mind.

'Your thanks were taken for granted,' he said. 'Many of our sheep have almost drowned, too. I've been out every day rounding them up. On horseback, mostly. The silly coots. Sheep haven't enough sense to come in out of the rain.'

He leaned forward and made a church steeple with his hands under his chin. 'The river's running pretty high at present; you wouldn't want to swim there now. Nor for weeks, months to come.'

She glanced down at the linoleum floor, aware that the barrier of estrangement was an obstacle she had no way of surmounting or bypassing. He was another man, a stranger, and she wanted to weep.

'I spoilt the day for you,' she said. 'I was as stupid as your sheep, Quentin.' She took a deep, steadying breath. 'I apologise sincerely. If I hadn't been so headstrong, if I'd taken heed of your warnings . . . That's why I wanted to see you, to say what I have just said now.'

He looked at her steadfastly, no emotion or expression registering on his tanned face. Then he gave a small awkward shrug of indifference.

'We all make a mistake or two. That's not your prerogative, Jancy.'

'I seem to have made more than one or two since moving into Bungalan.'

He did not answer, but turned his head to stare at the red and orange flames leaping up into the chimney over the massive fireplace.

Jancy couldn't stand this intolerable farce another moment, this polite and civilised pretence. Rejected, deflated, she accepted the obvious, that this unplanned meeting had run its course and reached a stalemate. Quentin had nothing to say to her, so why add humiliation to injury.

'Oh, well,' she said with a forced smile, disguising her wounded pride and disappointment. 'I thank you, anyway. Goodbye.'

8

There were other crises, each another strain and burden to carry. The load, and the road Jancy travelled, were getting rougher. Custom had fallen off alarmingly and her new-season stocks, despite increased advertising and commensurate expenditure, brought no response whatever.

Michael called a couple of times, after dark on each occasion. His caution, his attempts at discretion, so absurd in the light of general knowledge, no longer riled her and she did not comment. On both visits they had dinner together in the flat over the shop and the evenings were companionable, if becoming less compatible.

It was quite ridiculous; with every intention to demand a showdown, she found herself unable to deliver an ultimatum. Perhaps it was the fear of losing him completely; half a loaf or even a few crumbs being preferable to no bread at all.

When the knocking sounded on the front door and intuition warned her the caller would be Michael Rickwood — who else? she had few friends — she would steel herself and resolve to have it out with him before he left later in the evening.

But she didn't. The clasp of his hand, his arm held tenderly about her shoulders, the gentle, lingering kiss of welcome, and her firm intentions were demolished in adolescent gratitude for his presence, his sometime favours.

She was beginning to despise herself.

Aunt Edith Talliman, she knew, would have turned over in her grave at her niece's extraordinary lack of will-power, of mature common sense.

She knew, she *knew* what she was doing to herself and what Michael was doing, using her for his own amusement, keeping her dangling on a string of part-time affection. And yet, she was so weak, so idiotically weak and vulnerable. Really, her attitude to the whole situation was pathetic.

Did their love have to be so difficult, so wrenching, so tearing apart, she asked of herself over and over. And was it love or a simple manipulation of affection?

If only she had the strength of purpose to let go, send him away, to free him and, in the process, free herself. If she did this, and he went, there would be no one to take his place, no one to offer her a soft shoulder to lean on, a few precious hours of togetherness, of being wanted and needed.

Another problem was Susan Rickwood. One morning, Susan arrived at work, red-eyed and snuffling, to announce she was quitting her job.

Jancy should have been aware of trouble brewing, from Susan's behaviour in the days leading up to the resignation. There should have been premeditation. But she had been preoccupied and withdrawn, pale-faced, and under duress from a dozen mounting worries crowding her at one and the same time.

Sigrid had noticed something amiss and had briefly mentioned Susan's change in personality, but Jancy had ignored the warning signals, being totally involved in other matters.

The bad weather had broken, but it was still miserable and unsettled, with showers or storms every second day at least and the skies low and forbidding. Everything was damp and clammy indoors and the plains surrounding Bungalan were still covered with broad expanses of floodwater, unable to drain away. There hadn't been a fine, sunny day in more than a month.

The weather was adversely affecting trade, too. Barely a trickle of people were motoring to the coast and business was more than slack; it had taken a disconcerting downward plunge. Women customers were simply not venturing out and about, and who could blame them?

It was bound to pick up sooner or

later, Jancy kept reassuring herself, familiar with the foibles and unpredictable highs and lows of the rag trade. Sigrid was doing her best to maintain and boost morale, her blonde prettiness and perky moods brightening the gloom of empty days. But Jancy was deeply concerned, nonetheless. Financial commitments had to be met on their due date and wages paid, as well as the manufacturers' monthly accounts of stock delivered in the early autumn.

So when Susan came in, hang-dog in expression and clearly troubled, Jancy knew automatically it was going to be another of those tense and strained days.

'I can't work here any more,' Susan Rickwood announced dramatically, and straightaway burst into tears.

Jancy did her best to console the distraught girl, Sigrid also, but Susan was too upset to be comforted by kind and awkward platitudes.

'I have to leave,' she sobbed. 'There's

no option. I've thought about it and thought about it, and I can't give it up. Not when I've dreamed about it for years and years.'

'Give what up?' Jancy asked patiently, trying to get to the crux of the dilemma.

'A return air ticket to Europe,' Susan cried. 'Mother said she will pay all expenses for a six months' trip abroad, provided I leave the shop immediately.'

Jancy bit her lip at the outrageous bribe. 'Well, you can't pass that up,' she told the stricken girl, her expression grim. 'What a marvellous opportunity for you, dear. And we all know you've been saving like mad to get there under your own steam . . . '

'But . . . don't you see?' Susan gave her a beseeching look. 'She's done this deliberately, to force me to leave here. I love working in the boutique, Jancy. I really do. It made me independent. But I've dreamed of going abroad and every dollar I could get together I've banked . . . '

Jancy's brows lowered. 'Susan, dear, it's not the end of the world. Maybe this world, but there's a bigger, more exciting one overseas. The job here is relatively unimportant. You enjoyed it and I enjoyed having you. More important, I suppose, are the wishes of your mother.'

Then she asked: 'What does Quentin have to say about the sudden and extravagant offer?'

'Nothing.' Susan sniffed and blew her nose long and loud. 'Nothing at all. As if he doesn't care. And he always used to. Quentin's gone all peculiar, moping about the place, and a dozen girls phoning him up. He's no fun any more. We used to do mad things and have a ball, ganging up against the dragon, and Michael ... Michael doesn't care, either. Except about himself.'

Jancy flinched.

'Don't worry,' Sigrid Vigeland said soothingly, with an anxious glance at Jancy. 'I'd jump at such a chance. Can't imagine anyone offering me a free trip.

You couldn't possibly refuse it.'

Susan dabbed at her eyes with a lace handkerchief. 'Of course I can't. But it's wrong, she's making things impossible. I'm not a child. I was happy to help out at home, as well as holding down a job. What's wrong with that? Of course I want to travel, but not with strings attached. It's unfair and cruel and I feel terrible about it. Why can't I have a life of my own choosing and planning without interference?'

Jancy sighed. Why not, indeed! Did anyone have a life free from interference in one manner or another?

On the Friday morning following Susan's abrupt departure from the boutique Jancy hitched a lift into Canberra with young Peter Mason. Sigrid had told her he was driving into the federal capital and would be returning in the mid-afternoon.

The schedule suited Jancy, allowing her a few hours of leisure, and Peter was delighted to have the company of a passenger. She had phoned for an appointment with both the bank manager and her accountant to learn, in the event of a final and irrevocable decision to burn her bridges at Bungalan, how she would be situated financially.

Fortunately, it was another of the occasional on-and-off days they had enjoyed without rain, though the threat of it had been omnipresent since daybreak. The sun was a mere glimmer through a grey sky and, unimpressed by the promise of a break in the weather, Jancy took her raincoat and umbrella.

The road into Canberra had deteriorated rapidly, though it was nowhere as bad or hazardous to driving as the secondary road to Warabee. The journey passed quickly enough and it seemed no time at all before Peter had reached his destination and let her out of the vehicle at a corner near the Civic Centre.

As soon as Jancy was announced to the bank manager he made himself available, and within minutes her debit and credit affairs were presented in concise and explicit detail.

To Jancy's relief, she was much better off than she had realised. The overdraft was being reduced at double the rate she had originally considered prudent when the boutique first opened and, as the bank manager pointed out, she had also gained the benefit of a considerable profit in goodwill, an intangible asset at present but important if and when she decided to sell out.

She left the bank half an hour later and after subsequent discussions with her accountant found herself in a mood of elation. In fact, she felt happier and more relaxed than she had in weeks past.

The good news from both sources put an entirely different interpretation on things. Despite misgiving, she had made a success of Jancy's Boutique after all, facts and figures proved that, and pride in the accomplishment, not to mention the accountant's flattery concerning her business acumen, made the dull day almost rainbow-hued.

And with those feelings buoyantly swinging her along one of the main shopping streets in the centre, she met Michael Rickwood face to face.

'Hello, there,' he greeted affably, his handsome features breaking into a smile of pleasure at the sight of her. He took her arm and gave it an affectionate squeeze. 'What brings you this far from home?'

'Dollars and cents,' she told him lightly. 'I've been checking on the affairs of the business.'

'I'm sure they're healthy, with you at the reins.'

'Well,' she countered, 'the boutique is not exactly galloping at present, but neither is it a dead horse. Let's say it was doing, until recently, a profitable canter. I think I can coast along for a while yet without getting into deep water. This weather hasn't helped, of course.'

He laughed. 'You look marvellous today. There's a sparkle in your eyes. I noticed the instant I caught sight of you. And that English rose complexion, all pink and glowing from the cold . . . '

'Take another look,' Jancy retorted with gaiety. 'The skin has chafed and freckled. The rose is full-blown.'

'Nonsense.' He clasped her hand possessively and drew her along the crowded street with him. 'How about an early lunch? It's close to midday and I'm famished. Can I tempt you?'

'When didn't you tempt me?' she asked with a shrug, and a smile to remove the unintentional barb.

'In that case . . . ' The comment did not even register. 'We'll have wine as well.'

The restaurant he chose was on the second floor of a multi-storey building, the spacious dining room decorated in Spanish motifs of red, gold and black.

It was very Mediterranean, elegant and sophisticated. And no doubt very expensive, if the elaborate covers containing the menus and wine lists were any indication.

They were shown to a tête-à-tête

table near the front windows that overlooked a park, and as soon as they were seated Michael said: 'Too bad about Susan taking off and leaving your employ. But she's had her heart set on going abroad for a long time, as you were probably aware. It was no secret to anyone.'

'No, she certainly spread it around,' Jancy admitted. 'I'll miss her, of course, but I have a replacement.' Which was not strictly true; she was only in the process of finding a replacement.

'She'll enjoy London very much,' Michael went on. 'I know I did.' His smile was conspiratorial, to stir old memories. 'Didn't we?'

Jancy spread a napkin across her lap, choosing not to be stirred. 'It all seems so long ago.'

'Not to me.' Michael shook his head. 'I can remember everything, as if they happened yesterday.'

'But they didn't,' Jancy reminded him quietly and effectively. 'I've been too busy to wear those kinds of yesterdays on my sleeve. I'm afraid, since I came to Bungalan, I'm more concerned with tomorrows.'

Michael gave her a quizzical glance, a slight frown of disapproval. Then the waitress came up, Jancy ordered and, as Michael deliberated on his choice of meal, looked at him with veiled appraisal.

He was wearing a brown houndstooth jacket and a white polo-neck sweater. His skin was brown and his hair black and thick, a stray lock falling boyishly over his forehead. Unobserved by him, she stared contemplatively at the wide, sensuous mouth, the cleft chin, the glint of perfect teeth through his half-open mouth.

A perfect specimen, he was almost too handsome. And too arrogant and mocking. To capture such a prize would be like trying to harness a cyclone, if an immovable force could be considered a prize. Through marriage he would do as he pleased, go where he pleased, when he pleased. Joy in the morning would turn soon enough to anguish in the evening.

She thought, surprised by her own candid evaluation: Was he really like that back home, miles across the sea? Was he always so selfish, self-contained, conceited? So wrapped in his own ambitious schemes and purposes? Was I so blind, so smitten, I was unable to see the wood for the trees, the shadow instead of the substance?

The image was blurring about the edges and suddenly Jancy felt a surge of melancholy. Then she had a curious feeling that someone was watching her and, discomfited by the awareness, she turned her head to survey the restaurant.

Across the room a middle-aged woman in a red velvet turban waved a greeting.

There was no mistaking Jancy was the object of the attention, and she nodded an acknowledgement. The face, the well-padded figure were familiar, but the name eluded her.

'Someone you know?' Michael asked casually as the waitress hurried off with the orders.

'Not actually,' Jancy corrected. 'Someone I met briefly at the drive-in cinema.' She smiled at the woman, whom she now recalled had been very pleasant, and Michael followed the direction of her eyes.

'That's Grace Franklin,' he said with a frown. 'A good friend of Cynthia's.'

Jancy grimaced slightly, unconcerned. 'For my untarnished reputation — is that good or bad?' She was teasing him, of course, but irony lurked behind the flippant question.

'I doubt if she's a gossip.' Michael rubbed his chin reflectively as if the woman's presence had ruffled him slightly. Why should it, Jancy pondered. He brought me here, in public view.

'But who cares?' Michael gave an abrupt laugh, to dismiss the awkward predicament. 'I'm lunching with a very attractive young woman and I'm probably the envy of every other man in the dining room. I doubt whether Cynthia will demand or expect an explanation.'

Jancy toyed with a fork, wishing they had gone to some lesser restaurant elsewhere. How much longer would she have to tolerate this back-street relationship?

'I bet she wouldn't get it, even if she does,' Jancy said. 'In the innocent circumstances . . . '

'My luncheon dates are my own affair,' Michael stated with a twist of his shoulders, rationalising his own position. 'For all Grace Franklin knows we could be discussing a property deal. You could be selling me a couple of stud rams, or half a hundred prime ewes. Or a parcel of land.'

Jancy gazed at him with growing irritation. 'Except that she knows I'm the owner of a boutique and not a stock and station agent.'

'Don't fret.' Michael tried to placate her by deliberately clasping her hand across the table. For Grace Franklin's benefit. 'I'm a big boy, and responsible only to myself. Maybe we should invite the good woman over and ask her to share a bottle of wine with us.'

Jancy shook her head. 'You're pressing your luck, big boy.'

'That's the name of the game, Jancy. Living dangerously. You should realise that; you're a player.'

That did it. Jancy's formerly light and buoyant mood evaporated. The restaurant was beautifully appointed and the food and service excellent, but Jancy couldn't wait for the meal to end and to make her departure.

She had arranged to meet Peter Mason at three o'clock for the return trip to Bungalan and wanted an hour to herself in which to do bits and pieces of personal shopping.

Michael seemed reluctant to part company. Almost deliberately he dawdled over the dessert, deciding on a second cup of coffee, and the hour she had assumed the luncheon would take stretched interminably into close on two.

Finally, out in the street, she managed to separate from him and lose herself in the crowd thronging a nearby department store.

She returned to the parked car ten minutes before the scheduled time and found Peter already seated behind the wheel.

'Have a good day?' he asked, swinging open the passenger door. She climbed in beside him, stacking her parcels on her lap.

'Not too bad. And you?'

'Mission accomplished.' Peter gestured through the windscreen at the threatening sky. 'We're in for a stormy trip home. Care to invest some money in building an ark? Accommodation guaranteed.'

Preoccupied with Michael and a post mortem on the luncheon, she hadn't noticed the marked change in the weather. Thunder clouds reared over the hills ahead of them, black and forbidding.

'No more rain, surely,' Jancy answered

in dejection. 'We'll all be growing webbed feet soon.'

'If that's a prophecy,' Peter told her with a grin, 'it might well come true. But I'll settle for a boat every time. A week's solid rain, on top of what we've had, and I reckon we'll be in trouble. There's been too much flooding already in parts of the district. And it's going to get worse before it gets better.'

The storm broke as they sped through the outskirts of Canberra, heading for their distant village.

Giant thunderclaps shook the earth and spears of lightning rent the angry sky. Then the rain fell, in torrents, drenching the countryside and restricting visibility to a few hundred feet. Even on maximum speed the windscreen wipers were unable to cope with the incredible downpour.

Peter changed down to low gear and finally, for safety's sake, pulled over to the side of the road and switched off the wipers.

It would be wiser, he said, to leave

the engine running. If he turned it off they might not get started again. The rain flooded over them, swilling down the windows. They couldn't see a thing outside. Vision was completely obliterated.

Then, to make light of the situation and leaning back in his seat, Peter drawled: 'Care for a cup of coffee while we're waiting?'

Jancy mused on the invitation, appreciating the young man's effort to help her relax. 'Well, if we're going to be stuck here indefinitely . . . yes, I'll have a cup, with cream and two sugar cubes.'

To her surprise and amusement he actually did have coffee on hand, in a cane-woven picnic hamper on the back seat. With a chuckle he reached over, opened the hamper and produced a thermos of coffee which he poured, with exaggerated delicacy, into two plastic cups.

'Sorry about the cream. You can have it black with sugar, or black without.'

As they sipped the steaming liquid and felt it warming their chilled bodies, Peter said with studied nonchalance: 'Now that Susan Rickwood's gone and if you wanted to hire another sales assistant, I know a girl who might suit you.'

Was she a personal friend, Jancy asked.

He chuckled. 'Hardly. My cousin.'

Jancy said warily: 'I'll keep it in mind. Not that there's anyone else,' she hastened to add at the ripple of disappointment that crossed his face. 'Right now, business is not exactly booming out in the backblocks of Bungalan. We depend a great deal, as you probably realise, on passing trade.' She smiled ruefully. 'In recent weeks more ducks have gone by than people.'

'Well, her name's Marianne Sedley. For your information she's eighteen and has a terrific figure.'

'That's a consideration, when you're selling clothes,' Jancy said, and finished her coffee.

It was a slow and nerve-racking journey back to the village, on asphalt roads awash, and on each side pastures turning into shallow lagoons.

The storm and its intensity were the worst Jancy had ever experienced and, without voicing her apprehensions, doubted the wisdom of driving through it. As well, a violent wind had sprung up, and buffeted and lashed the vehicle with such ferocity that on several occasions Jancy feared they would be blown into a ditch or head-on into the low rows of trees that bordered the road here and there.

Despite his youth, however, Peter did not take unnecessary risks and his progress in such appalling conditions was admirably cautious.

Jancy couldn't wait to get back to the shop and her flat, and out of the wind-howling, rain-drenched storm. She was not normally nervous in inclement weather, and heaven only knew, she had been through enough snow-storms and slush and ice in winter England.

But this was different. With fences half-submerged and the entire landscape slowly being drowned, the forces of nature almost overwhelmed them in the immensity and destruction of its onslaught.

They barely spoke on the rest of the journey home. Peter concentrated on his driving, hunched forward to peer through the smeared windscreen. The only assistance Jancy could give was not to distract him.

So it was with tremendous relief that the village came into view through the grey curtain of rain, and, ahead, the enormous psychedelic sign announcing her boutique colourfully welcomed them back to shelter.

As Peter pulled up outside the shop and blew the horn, Sigrid came running out with an umbrella.

'What a dreadful afternoon!' she greeted, helping Jancy with the parcels. 'I wondered if you might have waited until it passed over.'

'By the looks of the weather,' Jancy said, 'we might have been waiting on the roadside for days. And become the talk of the town.'

The main street, with the pelting, wind-tossed rain driving under the awnings, was no place for idle conversation. Sigrid simply blew Peter a kiss as he drove off and hustled Jancy into the calm and warmth of the boutique.

'We haven't had one solitary customer the whole afternoon,' Sigrid announced mournfully as Jancy slipped out of her jacket. She had her blonde hair drawn back into a pony tail with a gay red ribbon. The style was severe and her face looked thin and pale.

Jancy patted her arm. 'You were worried about us?'

'Terrified,' Sigrid admitted. 'I kept thinking the upstairs flat might come crashing down on top of me. Or, at least, the roof blown off. The wind was scary. And the rain's been beating in under the closed windows in the back room. I laid a towel across the sill to soak it up. Did you have much trouble in getting through? Was the road cut at all?'

'No, not yet.' Jancy shook her head. The road had been clear, though in some places floodwater had reached the shoulders of the bitumen.

'I've been listening to the radio,' Sigrid went on. 'They're issuing flood warnings again for the whole district. And there's something wrong at Warabee dam. I don't know what exactly, the statics on the radio were pretty bad. But I heard them mention the dam and how much water was pouring into it behind the wall and they can't get it away faster than it's flowing in.'

Anxiety made her blue eyes look feverish. 'Do you think my mother and father will be all right? And Arnie, and the others?'

'Of course,' Jancy reassured her, but with a germinating alarm of her own. 'If the news has been broadcast, then obviously everyone up at the construction site knows about it. If there's the slightest danger, the authorities are bound to evacuate them. Anyway,' she added, giving Sigrid a comforting hug, 'telephones are still operating. If there was any real problem I'm sure Mr and Mrs Vigeland or Arnulf would have got in touch with you. In this particular case I don't see how no news can be bad news.'

Though not fully convinced, Sigrid nodded doubtfully and gave her a wavering smile.

'Why don't we close up?' Jancy suggested. 'We'll both take the rest of the afternoon off. And anytime, if you feel like phoning the dam, by all means do so. There's no need to ask.'

'Then if you don't mind,' Sigrid said, 'I'll put a call through straight away . . .'

*　*　*

About ten o'clock on the Sunday morning Helena Rickwood cornered Michael in the study where he had busied himself with the monthly book-keeping accounts. A fireside-simulated electric heater made the room cheerful and cosy and he had been in the room for more than an hour, immersed in the affairs of Irongates.

Before confronting her elder son, Mrs Rickwood had established the whereabouts of her other children, not wanting them to intrude on her personal talk.

Susan was in her own room, reading through a pile of travel brochures and dreaming of *la dolce vita* in European ports of call, and Quentin was down at the feed sheds with several of the hired hands, shifting bags and bales of feed above floor level. They had lost a number of sheep, as had other property owners, but there was little they could do other than transfer the flocks to the highest points of the vast holding.

So, as planned, she had Michael entirely to herself when she strolled into the study and closed the door behind her.

'I have a very important matter to discuss with you,' she began, moving around his heavy mahogany desk to stand directly in front of him.

'If it concerns the weather,' Michael said wearily, 'it's out of my hands. Quentin's taken charge of the stock; he'll do the best he can.'

'Our increasing financial losses are bad enough,' his mother said crisply, her face composed though her hands, toying with the pearls at her throat were not. 'Who is Arnulf Vigeland?'

Michael put down the pen he had been using and slouched back in his leather chair, his brow furrowed partly by the interruption and partly by the question.

'I wouldn't have a clue. Am I supposed to?'

'I would strongly advise you to learn more about him, whoever the man may be. He was seriously injured in a car smash this morning — at five o'clock, to be precise — on the Sydney road.'

Michael made a gesture of impatience. 'Please get to the point,' he said sharply, accustomed to but seldom appreciating his mother's flair for dramatics.

Helena Rickwood stared at her son over the rims of her blue-framed spectacles. He was the first-born and held a special endearing place in her heart, but there were times when she detested his smugness, when she wanted to lash out at him for his wilful disregard of people and feelings. And that included herself.

Deep down she knew that she was responsible. They were two of a kind and she personally, through childhood and adolescence, had created the man he had become, with all his faults. One day, perhaps, armed with a strength of purpose and determination he had always lacked, he would connive to defy her authority, but not yet. She was still mistress of Irongates and he a well-paid and obedient servant.

'The point is,' Mrs Rickwood said

slowly, 'this Vigeland person had a passenger alongside him in the front seat. And that passenger was Cynthia Meddow.'

Michael laid his hands flat on the desk, his whole body stiffening. 'Is she . . . hurt?'

'A few bruises, and shock. Nothing serious. She was fortunate. The car, I believe, is almost a write-off.'

Michael visibly relaxed. He fingered the paisley cravat he wore, then slowly drew a cigarette from a packet on the desk and lit it, inhaling deeply.

Whatever his emotions, he was able to cover them up. 'How am I supposed to react to that bit of news, Mother?'

'The same as I reacted,' she retorted scathingly. 'With indignation, suspicion even. What was Cynthia — your intended wife — doing in the company of a strange man at that ungodly hour of the morning? If they were travelling, and that they were, where had they been since midnight? A tawdry affair at some sleazy highway motel?'

'No!' Michael said quietly. 'You're wrong.'

'Then consider the possibilities . . . '

Michael stared at his mother through slitted eyes. 'You're being cruel, doing Cynthia an injustice. Your accusations are based on pure supposition, without facts to substantiate them. How can you possibly make such preposterous statements about Cynthia, of all people. She wouldn't, she couldn't be a party to . . . '

Helena Rickwood held up an imperious hand.

'As an intelligent woman, and of the same sex, I am capable of assuming the obvious. There is much more to it. I have heard rumours and so must you, even if you chose to ignore them — that Cynthia has been seen in the company of another man. He's a construction worker at Warabee dam, I believe; I made it my business to ascertain his position. Imagine!'

She threw her head back and gazed in mock despair at the ceiling or whatever was on high. 'Imagine! A wealthy, well-bred girl like Cynthia involving herself with a common labourer.'

Michael drew on his cigarette. 'Is he a labourer?'

'He's employed by the construction company and lives in barracks of some kind or another at the camp. Isn't that enough?'

'He could be a qualified engineer, with a university degree. Would that make him more acceptable, a professional man?'

Helena Rickwood took a deep breath and her nostrils flared with anger. 'Don't you care about the girl you're going to marry, about her reputation?'

Michael shrugged. 'Where is Cynthia now?'

'She was taken to hospital and allowed to leave. She's home, at Peppertree, with her father. Whatever must he be thinking? He adores her . . . '

'If you've been in touch,' Michael

said drily, 'he's probably thinking the same as you, no doubt.'

'Don't be sarcastic,' Mrs Rickwood snapped. 'It's a characteristic you have I sometimes despise.'

She turned her back on her son and stared through the open slats of the venetian blind, looking out through the rain-smeared window at the wet and misty day. With this latest crisis it seemed almost as depressing in the study as it was out there, in the open paddocks.

'There's another matter, too,' she continued, turning back to the object of her maternal ire. 'You're not exactly the injured party in this unfortunate mess. Grace Franklin saw you in the Amiado Spanish restaurant in town, lunching with that . . . that Jancy Talliman. In a public place. In full view of all our friends. Are you mad, Michael? What kind of game are you playing, courting Cynthia one day, and the next playing around with a shopgirl?'

Helena Rickwood's social snobbery

was a family joke and as she ranted on Michael smiled thinly at her incredible, and disproportionate, sense of values. She was not the First Lady of Bungalan, but, by Harry, she had long worn the crown as such, a matriarch for the landed gentry.

He said, irritably stubbing the half-smoked cigarette in an ashtray: 'What I do in my own time is my own affair. I'm only one member of the Irongates clan. There's Quentin and Susan . . . '

Mrs Rickwood dismissed them both with an impatient wave. 'Susan has been brought to heel, by simple bribery, and as for Quentin — I've never been able to control that boy, so I ceased trying a long time ago.'

'Why not cease trying with me, Mother?'

'Because you're the Rickwood thoroughbred,' she answered, with passion throbbing in her voice. 'Of all my children, you're the one who will hold on to Irongates. I shouldn't be saying that — I love the others, too — but when I'm gone there has to be someone to make our land become more productive, more profitable. This land is our heritage.'

Michael lit another cigarette. 'And what if I reject your grand schemes, your plans for an alliance of families? My God, you've been working at it all my life that I can recall. I'm not a piece of clay, for you to mould. And this is not a stud farm we're running, with six little Rickwoods at yearly intervals . . .'

Helena Rickwood made a deprecating gesture. 'Think again,' she scoffed. 'Clay is exactly what you are. I've shaped you, fashioned you into the man you are today. Don't pretend with me, son. We're two of a kind. We take what we want. We plot — yes, that's the word — we plot and chart our lives for this year, next year, and even to the next generation.'

She was playing with her pearls again, and all at once the string snapped and the pearls scattered across the desk and the carpet at her feet.

They were given scant attention.

Ignoring the minor accident, she went on: 'You're fond of Cynthia, even if not head-over-heels in love. That's sufficient to start off a marriage.'

Michael said thoughtfully: 'I'm not exactly sure it is.'

His mother stared at him hard for a long time. 'Then I suggest you reassure yourself on that small point, for your own sake as well as mine. I am still the legal owner of Irongates, the lawful head of this house. Every acre, every blade of grass, every sheep out there, belongs to me. If you were disinherited . . .'

Pushing back his chair, Michael sprang to his feet, rising anger flushing his handsome face. 'Come off it, Mother. I won't be threatened . . .'

She shook her head. 'It's not a threat,' she answered. 'It's a solemn warning. Either you charm Cynthia into an immediate and formal engagement, with an early marriage — say, in three months' time — or I'll cut you off without a cent.'

Michael's eyes blazed in temper. 'You

wouldn't dare. I've worked hard on this property . . . '

'Hard!' Mrs Rickwood interrupted. 'You don't know the meaning of the word. Quentin works hard, day and night when necessary. But you're the playboy, the bookkeeper. You're bone lazy, my son. But I have to forgive you that, because I encouraged you to loaf and travel and sponge off the profits.'

'Mother!' Michael's voice rasped with fury. 'That's enough.'

'True,' she agreed. 'And now I have other things to do.' She took a final look through the venetian blind. 'We've had too much rain,' she said, as if talking to herself. 'I think we're about to have the worst flood in living memory.'

Without another glance at her son or the loose pearls at her feet, she walked from the room, leaving the door open behind her.

9

He came to see her on the Saturday morning at — for Michael — a most extraordinary hour. He had always been so meticulous in observing the proprieties, had there been cause to observe them, choosing after-dark visiting that permitted him to call without advertising his presence to the community.

On this occasion, however, it was not quite seven o'clock. Any other morning it was unlikely Jancy would have been up and about, but she had slept badly the previous night and had awakened at six-thirty in need of the stimulus of a cup of coffee.

She had been sitting on the edge of the bed, a red quilted dressing-gown wrapped snugly about her, when she heard a car door slam and, being in the right position at the right moment, idly checked on the vehicle through the bedroom window.

Astonishment almost caused her to drop the cup and saucer. Hastily putting them aside, she peered through the sheer white curtains to follow Michael's movements.

He was driving the Land-Rover which, in itself, was also unusual until it occurred to her that perhaps it was a more suitable vehicle, in wet weather, for traversing the gravel roads on the Irongates property.

It was still raining in a fine, unrelenting drizzle, and after he had slammed the driver's door Michael jogged across the rain-washed roadway towards the entrance to the boutique.

Again, to her surprise, Jancy found herself unexpectedly composed at the sight of him. Whatever Michael wanted, or wanted to tell her, it must have been desperately urgent. Whatever the crisis, she was prepared for it.

Automatically, as she quickly ran a comb through her sleep-tangled hair, her mind skipped over half a dozen possibilities. It did not take long to grasp the essential one, the only possible reason for this pre-breakfast call.

She waited several seconds until the doorbell rang, then went downstairs, through the shop, to answer it.

At the sight of him, feigning disbelief and her eyes wide, she exclaimed: 'Of all people . . . Good heavens, you must have been up with the sparrows. What time is it?'

'I know it's early,' Michael replied. 'But I see you're up and about. Can I come in, or do you propose keeping me out in the weather?'

His temper, she noted, was as bristly as his face. She had never seen him unshaven before, and the black stubble did nothing to enhance his appearance.

'The cobwebs haven't gone yet,' she soothed. 'Of course you can come in. I'm sorry.' She opened the door wide and he hurried past her, as if anxious to be out of sight of unseen, watchful eyes.

'Well, what's the trouble, Michael?'

she asked patiently.

'How about some coffee?' he parried. 'I'm half-frozen.'

'You have time to spare? You're not racing the clock? At this hour . . . '

He said, trailing her up the stairs and into the flat: 'Time enough. I may have to go to Melbourne later in the day, but I wanted to talk with you urgently before I left.'

'Sounds ominous,' she answered. Then, gaily: 'Talk away.' Already she had anticipated the reason for his visit and felt curiously unaffected by the intuitive knowledge. She knew the man well enough to understand, though not to appreciate, his diverse moods and his ways of talking in circles. It was one of his minor irritations, an inability to make a direct statement, or give a straightforward, uncomplicated answer to an important question.

As he parked himself at the kitchen table Jancy filled the electric jug and plugged it in. 'All I have is instant coffee . . . '

Michael rubbed his hands together to warm them. 'I'll settle for that. Make it hot and strong.'

'Double-strength coming up. You look as though you need it.'

As she had used hot water from the kitchen sink, the jug boiled almost immediately. Making the coffee, Jancy kept looking at him, striving to be patient and finding it a difficult job.

There you are, she thought, a quizzical smile lurking in the corners of her mouth. Big and strong, if not hot and strong, sitting there like a worried schoolboy, wanting to get the news off your manly chest and unable to tell me. Shall I tell you, instead?

You've come to say goodbye, my fancy. And that's all I've been, your fancy. Fancy Jancy. Goodbye, my darling, it was great knowing you.

And what you can't find the courage to say is that Arnie Vigeland and Cynthia were involved in a nasty accident, which in turn revealed an awkward situation, and the dragon lady is breathing fire and smoke down your neck.

So, along with Susan, you also have been given an ultimatum. Marry Cynthia and marry her quickly, or else. Unite the Rickwood property with the Meddow property in holy matrimony and you'll gain lots and lots of lovely land. Half the state. Well, near enough. It would appear that large.

'What's so amusing?' Michael demanded gruffly, aware of the scrutiny. 'You find amusement in me being here, for a cup of coffee?'

She placed the steaming mug in front of him, and a plate containing several biscuits.

'No, Michael. I was miles away, thinking of other things. Anyway — I realise you must have had a purpose in driving so early into the village, so why not unload the problem. I have . . . I've always had . . . a good shoulder to lean on.'

Michael sipped the coffee, frowning as the steam clouded up into his face.

Wishing he would get on with it, Jancy began to probe. 'Is it — about us, you and me?' The shop had to be opened at nine o'clock, customers or no customers, and she had a number of things to do before then.

'Yes,' he said, with deliberation. 'It concerns us both.'

'You sound,' she laughed, trying to make it easier for him, 'very serious.'

'It is serious. Extremely serious. And you're being flippant. Please don't joke.'

'I'm not joking,' she assured him, the smile ebbing away. 'I've known you long enough to be able to tell when something is disturbing you. Stop hedging, Michael, and get to the point.'

He shrugged. 'I'm not sure how to start. I'm rather nervous . . . '

With a sigh she said: 'Perhaps it might be better if I told you.'

He gave her a sullen look. 'Are you sure we're on the same tack?'

Jancy nodded. She was totally convinced. 'The same tack, the same road, the same federal highway. Arnulf Vigeland and Cynthia Meddow and their automobile accident.'

She had burst into tears when the news came through. Tears for Arnie, for a wonderful and loyal friend. Almost every day she had been in touch with the hospital, checking on his progress.

'Well . . . ' Michael said truculently. 'You appear to have it cut and dried. You know it all, or so you think.'

'I know enough. Bad news travels fast.' Jancy leaned back against the sink. 'How do you propose to handle the relationship between Arnie and Cynthia? Or is it the same old story? Do exactly nothing and hope it will sort itself out?'

'What would you have me do?' he countered, with an edge of sarcasm.

Very slowly, since her hands were starting to tremble with suppressed anger, she set down the cup.

'Haven't you already decided? Hasn't your mother decided? Family honour must be maintained. Is it to be a duel with Arnie in his hospital bed? Rolled bandages at ten paces . . . '

'Jancy!' Michael's voice held the cold steel of a knife. 'I don't appreciate vulgarity. That's not funny.'

Sweeping a strand of hair back from her forehead, Jancy retorted: 'It wasn't meant to be funny. It was meant to be cutting, sarcastic.' Then she burst out: 'I've had enough, Michael. I've grown weary of being the odd girl out. I simply don't care any more. Arnie's in hospital, seriously hurt. How does your pride compare to that? You and your mother and the Irongates business . . . I'm sick and tired of it. I'm tired of having a part-time romance with you, tired of secrecy, tired of your inability to make up your mind. You're the one and only original cake-eater, my friend. Maybe you think having two of us on a string is good for your ego. Well, I've got news for you, Michael. It's demoralising for mine.'

With downcast eyes, his dark face brooding, Michael kept on sipping his coffee. 'Have you quite finished?'

'I've barely begun,' she flung at him, thoroughly wound up. Moving away from the sink, she stood at the table opposite her visitor.

'When you pause for breath,' he went on stiffly, 'perhaps we can talk rationally.'

Her eyes flashed. For months this moment had been building up into a climax. 'We haven't talked rationally since our parting in Bayswater Road, twelve thousand miles from here. In my case, distance has not lent enchantment.'

'Jancy!' Michael said, and thumped the empty coffee mug on the table. 'Listen to me and stop your nonsense. I want to announce our engagement.'

She opened her mouth to make a suitable retort, then, as the words sank in, clamped it shut.

'That's right,' he went on, as if placating a spoilt and wilful child. 'With a diamond ring, to make it official. I'll throw a huge party, two hundred people or more, in a month's time. It'll be the event of the season, and Mother can go to hell.'

For a while she was unable to speak. Colour drained from her face, leaving it pale and taut. After all this time, after all her dreams, her hopes . . . It was too sudden, too shattering.

'When would you care to make it public?' Michael asked.

Shaking her head in confusion, she said: 'I'll have to check on my desk calendar.'

'Oh, come off it,' he growled irritably. 'Is that all you have to say to me?'

She felt weak, so weak her knees began to shake. Feeling like a robot, willing her numbed limbs to move, she pulled out a chair and sat down heavily.

'The truth is — I don't know what to say.'

'It's quite simple,' he said, flashing a smile of charm and encouragement. 'Yes or no.'

The proposal wasn't the least bit simple. It left her bewildered, uncertain and suspicious of his motives.

'I'll have to think about it,' she said. And, indeed, she did have to think very carefully about him and their future. For a long, long time she had waited for this hour of triumph, fabricating a make-believe picture of candlelight and togetherness, of Michael's lips on her lips, and the miraculous moment when he asked her to be his wife.

The picture had blurred somewhat in recent months; the image of love distorted, out of focus, in the circumstances involving them.

Yes, she definitely needed to think, with clarity and maturity.

'Give me five minutes,' she pleaded, reaching for his hand and clasping it. 'Until I dress. Indulge yourself in another mug of coffee, switch on the radio . . . I won't be long.'

She closed the bedroom door behind her and quickly changed out of her warm pyjamas into a cherry-red sweater with a polo neck and tartan slacks.

245

Then she sat in front of the dressing-table mirror and ran a brush through her long, honey-brown hair. She had to do something with her hands. And her heart was beating furiously.

What would Aunt Edith Talliman advise, she pondered, drawing on memories. Accept the proposal, become one of the Irongates Rickwoods, change into a country socialite . . . ?

She stared at her sombre reflection in the mirror and gave a wan half-smile at the absurdity of her thoughts.

Aunt Edith couldn't help her now. And never in a million years would she be accepted into the landed gentry. Her background, her attitudes to snobbery would prevent her from attaining that illustrious peak on the social scale.

But why — and this was the most important, the most perplexing question — why had Michael asked her to be engaged, to marry him? She amended that; the word 'marriage' had not been mentioned, not once, in the conversation.

She toyed with that word, that lapse in speech, the brush moving slower and slower through her hair. Why? Why? He had professed, indirectly, ambiguously, to love and honour and cherish her. But all he was offering was a diamond engagement ring, nowhere as legal, as binding, as a wedding ring.

Then why?

Unless . . . unless it was a calculated attempt on Michael's part to bring Cynthia to heel. A last desperate attempt. If he knew about Arnulf and Cynthia, then certainly Helena Rickwood would be aware of the situation also. And if Mrs Rickwood started twisting her elder son's arm . . . Too long she had planned the merger, the union of Irongates and Peppertree. It had become her life's ambition, a dedication almost, for Michael to marry property and that property to pass on to descendants.

An engagement was one thing, but what if Michael's plans misfired? What if, through stubbornness and pride, he actually did lead her to the altar?

Jancy shook her head impatiently, trying to clear her thoughts and arrange them in a coherent pattern.

An engagement could be broken. Suppose Michael was using her as a lever to prise Cynthia free of Arnie? Obviously, Cynthia had her own rebellious ideas on a Peppertree — Irongates partnership. Unless her father started exerting pressure, as Helena Rickwood had been exerting it these months past.

'Michael,' she said aloud to her troubled reflection in the mirror, 'you don't really want to marry me. And in honesty, I don't really want to marry you. Come to think of it,' she added, straightening her sagging shoulders and feeling a burden lifted from them, 'I'm rather relieved it has worked out this way. We've been interludes in each other's life, that's all; an amusement, even an emotional leaning post.

'I'm convinced, Michael Rickwood, that being married to you would be the silliest mistake a girl could make. And if

Cynthia doesn't want you, and I don't want you, then you're out on a long limb of rejection.'

For a few moments she did not hear the voice of urgency coming from the small transistor radio she had on the buffet in the dining-kitchen.

As she opened the bedroom door, ready to face Michael and tell him of her decision, all she was conscious of was Michael's stance, half-leaning over the radio to catch every single word from the announcer, and the stunned expression on his face.

'What is it?' she asked in alarm. 'Whatever's wrong, Michael?'

He turned slowly, his voice soft and shocked.

'It's the Warabee dam,' he said. 'The wall's about to collapse and there's nothing in the world they can do to prevent it.'

10

The Warabee dam was breached at 8.24 a.m.

For more than a week past construction authorities, with growing concern but reluctant to make public the reasons for their increasingly frequent inspections, had visited the dam.

In the camp itself there had been a great deal of talk and speculation, with subsequent tension and alarm among the workmen and their families.

The private meetings they held, and the grim-faced assessments they made, were behind closed doors, the top brass including construction engineers and company executives. But closed doors or not, word began to leak out that all was not well at Warabee.

The long drawn-out winter rains had broken weather records for decades past. The rains had not only unseasonably filled the lake in the valley basin behind the earthen wall, but the pumping station and system had been plagued by breakdowns and electrical faults. Finally, overworked and operating inefficiently, the release outlet had been unable to cope with what should have been a regulated flow.

The huge volume of floodwater running off the hills miles behind the dam simply added its millions of muddy gallons to those already stored behind the sloping wall. Another factor in the inevitability of the disaster was that the continuity of the inclement weather had seriously hampered progress; the wall project was months behind schedule. Had it been twenty or thirty feet higher, the dam might never have broken.

Late on the Friday night fractures began to open up on the plains side of the dam wall and the general alarm was sounded. It was the worst possible time. Television programmes had long ended for the night and the only remaining source of general mass communication was by radio.

Comfortable and snug in their beds, few people heard the frantic warnings given out by the local radio network.

About two o'clock the Civil Defence organisation, alerted earlier, swung into full stride. The workmen and their families resident at the damp camp were hastily evacuated, though the camp itself, sited high on the slope, was well beyond reach of the lake waters.

And below the dam, where the real danger lay, hundreds of volunteers fanned out in every direction across the flat and open countryside, warning property owners by telephone or calling on them personally with frantic instructions to pack a few things and head for the shelter of high ground.

So, by dawn, a grey rain-drenched dawn that barely distinguished night from day, and beyond the radius of the path of the dam waters, only a small percentage of the population was aware of the imminent disaster.

For a few moments after Michael had run from the flat, clattering down the stairs and through the shop and speeding back to Irongates in a burn of wet rubber, Jancy Talliman was in a state of absolute panic.

In her mind's eye she could picture the catastrophe to come, a giant landlocked tidal wave of foaming, churning water released from captivity, pouring in a thunder through the breach in the dam and racing out across the plains. The lowlands were waterlogged already, their absorption capacity reached weeks ago when minor flooding had started throughout the district. Rivers were swollen and bursting their banks, farmland inundated, secondary roads blocked, causeways impassable or destroyed.

And now, added to this, the entire volume of water in the lake loosed upon the countryside.

It was a frightening image. Even

more frightening was another, more personal picture, in close-up, floodwaters pouring into Bungalan and the shop itself, spreading across the new carpets and rising higher and higher up the beautifully papered walls.

Time became precious. There was not a second to waste. But how fortunate she was; unlike many of the business premises fronting the main street, the boutique had upstairs accommodation. At least she would be able to salvage her stock, or part of it.

Without another second's delay Jancy ran downstairs, taking them two at a time, and threw open the front door Michael had slammed shut on the way out. She didn't dare waste even five minutes rushing up the street to the Empire Hotel to get Sigrid.

If Sigrid knew about the dam she would be frantic, thinking of the safety and welfare of her parents. And Mrs Mason or Peter wouldn't be of much help, either; she couldn't depend on them or expect assistance. They would have problems and worries of their own, trying to protect their households and personal belongings.

In the shop the carpeting and other fixtures were expendable; the stock was not.

Jancy hadn't realised she had so much of it, so many garments, in the boutique, in the back room, such a vast quantity of merchandise. Most of it should have been sold, and would have been sold in normal circumstances.

She could carry only so much in her arms at one time, and after a dozen hurried trips up the stairs, throwing clothing and other items wherever she found available space, she found her legs shaking from a combination of exhaustion and nervous strain.

Each time she raced downstairs to collect another armful, her eyes swept over the interior of the shop in a quick appraisal of which items to take next. To her dismay, even after a dozen trips, she did not appear to have made much impression at all.

Despite the urgency, however, Jancy had a practical nature. The feelings of panic and aloneness notwithstanding, and faced with the realisation she was entirely dependent on herself and her own resources, she was able to evolve a sensible system. The lower shelves of the display cases were given priority, then the racks of top-price dresses.

After twenty wearying ascents and descents of the monstrous stairs she was hastening back when one leg gave under her and with a cry of distress she tumbled and fell heavily down the last seven or eight steps.

Bruised and shaken, her hair spilling about her face and half-blinding her, she lay sprawled on the carpet, one leg doubled up under her body.

For long moments she remained in a heap, immobile, breathing heavily, until the spasms of shock ebbed away. Then carefully, terrified she had broken a bone or otherwise injured herself, she slowly worked herself into a sitting position. Her arms appeared undamaged, her legs too, but the right ankle began to throb painfully.

'Oh, blast!' she thought with despair, angrily knuckling a few tears from her eyes. What's wrong there? Of all times to have an accident.

Gingerly she pressed the skin and found the ankle almost too tender to touch.

It's sprained, she thought, furious with herself for being careless. Oh, blast, blast, blast!

She was about to get up, to hobble upstairs and bandage the limb, when she heard raised voices in the street, men shouting and loud splashing sounds.

And then, to her horror, from her position on the floor as she stared through the open doorway, she saw water starting to creep across the pavement.

She had known it would come, sooner or later, but the sight of that muddy water insidiously spreading was a chilling and paralysing sight.

She thought: It's here, already. And that means — the dam is broken, busted, the wall gone. It happened. And the flood has spread across the plain. It's in Bungalan, on the doorstep.

Her face ashen, her heart pumping violently and the throbbing ankle making her feel almost sick, she got to her feet and hobbled through the boutique to the front door. If she closed it, and laid towels behind both doors, perhaps it would give her a temporary reprieve, lessen the rate of flow into the premises.

But before closing the door she glanced outside. In the street the scene was incredible. An unbroken stretch of floodwater completely covered the roadway and footpaths, obliterating them. As she stared at the water, mesmerised by the extent of it, a solitary car travelled sluggishly along the crown of the road, creating foamcrested waves in its wake.

Then someone called, 'Jancy! Jancy!' and she stepped out into the swirling flood to see who it was.

Sigrid Vigeland came half-running, half-splashing along the pavement, dressed in long boots and a bright orange raincoat.

Jancy waved and Sigrid acknowledged it with a flashing smile.

'Water, water everywhere,' the girl announced unnecessarily as she drew closer. 'And it'll get worse. The radio's giving half-hour bulletins. They're expecting the water to rise to four or five feet in the village.'

Reaching the front doors of the boutique, she peered inside. 'Oh, the beautiful carpet,' Sigrid wailed. 'It will be ruined.'

'I can't help that,' Jancy told her. 'I'm more concerned about the stock, moving it upstairs.'

'Well, I'm here now,' Sigrid told her. 'Four hands are better than two.'

'Three legs, three good legs are a bit awkward.'

Sigrid's encouraging smile faded. 'What do you mean, Jancy? Three legs.'

Jancy grimaced and pointed to her right ankle. Hidden by the tartan slacks, it was beginning to swell.

'I tumbled down the stairs and twisted my ankle.'

'What a shame! Does it hurt much?'

Jancy put on a brave front. 'Not too much.'

'It'll hurt more later on,' Sigrid warned. 'So we had better do something about it straight away. Can you manage to climb the stairs?'

Jancy nodded. 'I don't have a choice, really. I'll have to.'

'That's the spirit.'

Then, because other things were more important than a sprained ankle, Jancy said: 'Your parents are safe and sound? They managed to get away from the camp?'

'They were given plenty of notice. They drove straight to Bungalan. Mother's at the hotel, sleeping in. She had such a night. You can imagine the flap that went on. My father is with her. Mr Fowler gave them a nice room, but

I can't remember whether it's the blue room, the pink or the green. Anyway, they'll be along presently, to help us.'

'But . . . they're not young,' Jancy protested. 'I can't expect them . . . They'll need rest.'

Sigrid shrugged. 'My people are strong, and strong-willed. When they decide to do something, it is as good as done. They will come soon. My mother said so.'

Then, without further delay, Sigrid insisted that Jancy lean on her for support and that the ankle be attended to immediately. In the bedroom the Norwegian girl helped Jancy remove the tartan slacks — 'They're already getting waterlogged,' she pointed out — and bound the swollen ankle.

Jancy was more than grateful for the attention and moral support, and impressed by her skill in first aid. It rather surprised her, in fact, to suddenly realise how efficient she was in other matters as well.

Before helping Jancy up the stairs she

had run into the back room, grabbed a couple of towels from a rack beside the wash-basin and used the towels to plug the gap between the carpet and the base of the front doors.

It was an emergency measure only; no matter what they did, the rising floodwaters would gain entrance sooner or later. But for the present, it allowed a brief respite.

After the ankle had been bandaged Jancy slipped into a warm skirt and zippered boots.

'At least they'll keep the bandage dry and support the leg,' Jancy said as Sigrid carefully closed the zippers. 'Thank you, Nurse Vigeland.' Then she added: 'I can't allow a silly accident to slow me down to a standstill. The stock has to be shifted. You know, I've lost track of the number of times I've raced up and down that staircase.'

In the ten minutes they spent upstairs the water had begun to force its way into the premises. On their return to the ground floor they found the towels not only saturated, but forced several inches back from the doors by the pressure of the flood outside. Most of the carpeting was soaking wet and around the showcase closest to the back room, where the floorboards slanted to a slight angle, spread a widening pool at least an inch deep.

Without wasting another moment, Jancy gave her assistant hurried instructions on transferring the stock. Lower shelving first, then the quality merchandise.

'If the radio reports are accurate,' Jancy said, 'practically everything will have to be moved.' They had tuned in to the broadcasts while the leg was being bandaged. 'They predicted a height of five feet in Bungalan and that's more than halfway up the walls. So everything, every single item, will have to be moved.'

But even with Sigrid's capable and energetic help they realised they were racing the clock. The back room was stacked with dozens of cartons, knitted goods and other items of clothing Jancy had not been able to shift because of the frightful weather. These, too, had to be manhandled from the rear premises, which was also the sewing room, into the main body of the boutique and up the stairs.

Although each load took only a few minutes — and the situation in the flat was growing more and more chaotic — correspondingly the floodwater was rising higher and higher. It was now almost six inches deep, swirling in eddies and currents between the restricting walls and pouring into the back room as well.

The physical wear and tear soon began to take its tolls. Jancy's ankle was growing worse, but she gritted her teeth and hobbled on. The situation was alarming, with a number of cardboard boxes already waterlogged and their contents ruined.

So she was overwhelmingly relieved and grateful when a loud knocking sounded on the front door, heralding the arrival of the Vigelands.

As Jancy limped to the door, pulled the useless towels away and opened up, the street water surged in a cascade into the premises.

'Sorry we are late,' Martin Vigeland apologised, ushering his wife inside and using his male strength to close the door again against the weight and volume of the flood. 'It was such a long night . . . '

'And a nightmare drive into the village,' Selma Vigeland added, giving Jancy an affectionate peck on the cheek. 'The road was bad, so bad. And Father was afraid to drive too fast in case of an accident.'

Her husband nodded. 'And afraid to drive too slowly in case a giant wave of water was chasing after us. It was a relief when we reached the hotel.'

'I suppose Samuel Fowler is also paddling about in water.'

'Oh, no.' Sigrid's mother shook her head. 'The hotel is built up, four or five steps from the street level. And it has not reached the top step. He is very fortunate, is the hotelkeeper. All his rooms filled with people from the dam and the only place in Bungalan with a floor still dry. Now,' she went on briskly, removing her warm gloves and a thick woollen scarf from around her neck. 'To work, yes? We fetch and carry and move everything up top. Is that not right?'

'It is right,' Jancy said, feeling humble. They were such open-hearted and generous people. Since the first meeting they had given her comfort and support. They had helped with the grand opening of Jancy's boutique and here they were again, working side by side with her in another desperate hour. And Arnulf would have been with them, she knew, had he not been confined to hospital.

The extra willing hands made a tremendous difference. As Sigrid had intimated, her mother was strong and untiring, a woman accustomed to domestic labours. She went up and down the stairs a score of times without apparent effort or fatigue.

But even though, collectively, they appeared to be coping with the stock in transferring it to the top floor of the building, the rising water was insidiously keeping pace with them.

Once, to rest the savagely aching ankle, Jancy looked through the bedroom window to see the full extent of the flooding. The sight had all the qualities of a disturbing dream. As far as the eye could see, in the cold grey morning light, the land was one vast inland sea of muddy water that stretched to infinity. In the aquatic desolation, houses stood alone and isolated. There was scarcely a person in view. Nothing moved, except the flow of the flood.

As she looked out, held captive by the incredible scene and the enormity of the destruction, she saw a householder a street back from the commercial centre hanging clothes on a makeshift line stretched along the front verandah. At the other end of the verandah several children huddled together, making paper boats and launching them upon the currents.

I'm glad someone's enjoying the catastrophe, Jancy thought. There will be a lot of heartbreak and financial ruin in this longest day.

Then she hurried back downstairs, as fast as her injured limb would allow, to do her share of the lifting and moving.

Within an hour the water was two feet deep in the boutique and sloshing over the tops of the boots Jancy and Sigrid were wearing. Finally, as the ankle began to swell, Jancy was forced to stagger upstairs again and remove the boot.

'Now you stay up there, where it is dry, and rest,' Selma Vigeland scolded. 'You hear, Jancy Talliman?'

'I hear,' she answered, appreciating the motherly concern. But she couldn't allow them to be wading about in cold and dirty water, to protect her business, while she remained idle. As much as the sprained ankle hurt, she had to shoulder some of the load.

When she came down again, prepared to work beside her friends, Mrs Vigeland shook her head in mock annoyance.

'We are managing very well, my dear. There is no cause for worry. Everything, or almost everything, is rescued, no? All the pretty dresses out of harm's way. We are very lucky, I think.'

'I'm the lucky one,' Jancy told her, 'to have such marvellous friends.'

'It is nothing. What else is there for us to do? We help each other in good times and bad. But,' and her voice was gentle, 'I understand how it is, why you must work too. It is important. So just do what you can.'

Martin Vigeland was magnificent, carrying twice as much as anyone else and practically leaping up and down the stairs. But even with the greater portion of her merchandise saved from the floodwaters, it was difficult not to feel despondent by the ravages of the water itself.

The carpeting was ruined, covered with inches of mud, and the beautiful wallpaper up to and beyond the water level was a sodden mess. The surging, swirling water filled the display- and show-cases and was rapidly reaching the heavy-duty sewing-mechine on the work table in the back room. The machine was too heavy to move manually and had to remain where it was. If that became submerged it would be a total loss.

For a while, biting her lower lip, she sat on the stairs above the water line, resting the ankle and allowing enough room for the others to pass.

Observing Jancy's quiet despair, Selma paused long enough to sit briefly beside her and place a comforting arm about her shoulders.

'It is bad, I know. But for others, much worse. Many people will suffer and perhaps lose everything.'

Jancy said: 'Never in my wildest dreams did I expect this kind of disaster.'

'Disaster?' Mrs Vigeland repeated. 'Not here, Jancy. Goodness me . . . All you have lost is floor covering, wallpaper and paint. It all looks so miserable now, I know, but when the flooding is past and we get to it with fresh water and scrubbing brushes and brooms and lots of soap, the shop will be as attractive as it ever was.'

Jancy's eyes began to fill.

'I think you are rather fortunate,' Selma Vigeland went on. 'Other people in the district, in the village, on the farms, will have had disasters; their furniture, their land, their houses, their worldly possessions ruined. I think we will count your blessings, my dear.'

Jancy nodded and impulsively kissed the older woman on the cheek. Aunt Edith might have told me that, she reasoned, ashamed her own selfish thoughts had been so apparent. Yes, Aunt Edith Talliman would have stirred her into an awareness, an appreciation, a gratitude of what had been accomplished. Aunt Edith would have pointed out the bright side of the situation.

Fifteen minutes later all the stock had been transferred upstairs into the flat and the four of them sat on the stairs, watching the restless ebb and flow of the floodwaters in the boutique.

'Once it reaches its peak it will go down swiftly,' Martin Vigeland predicted.

'And then we can start mopping up,' Sigrid added. 'Peter might help, too.'

'He has his own family,' Jancy pointed out. 'I couldn't allow that.'

The front doors were open and all at once the tall, lean figure of a man stood in the entrance, the floodwaters swirling about his legs.

'Are you there, Jancy Talliman?'

Michael! Jancy thought wildly, struggling to her feet and hanging on to the banister. It's Michael, and he's come back. But it wasn't Michael. It was Quentin Rickwood.

'I'm here,' she answered. 'With the Vigelands.'

He waded into the shop, foaming the

brown water as he ploughed through it.

At the foot of the stairs he looked up at them, the weary quartet, and smiled. 'Hello, everybody. Good weather for ducks.' Then he glanced about the empty premises. 'I assume all the merchandise has been salvaged and you won't be having a flood-damaged sale tomorrow. Half-price and under.'

'No,' she answered. 'My good friends, these wonderful helpers . . . '

She couldn't go on. None of this seemed real. The boutique turned into a filthy swimming pool, the wallpaper peeling and stained, her ankle throbbing worse than a toothache. And, in front of her, the last person in the world she expected to come calling.

She said, choosing the words carefully because she was close to breaking down in tears: 'What . . . what brings you into Bungalan, with the countryside overflowing? How did you get here, Quentin?'

He told her. In answer to the first question: to be of assistance at the shop. In answer to the second, he rode. And tethered the horse on the back verandah of the pub. The verandah boards were still above water level.

Jancy couldn't believe her ears. 'You rode — all that way from Irongates?'

'I couldn't drive,' he said with a deprecating shrug. 'How else could I have made it?'

She gulped, aware in the silence that none of the Vigelands was contributing to the conversation. 'But . . . your own place. The property . . . '

'The homestead is above flood level. There was nothing I could do; everything possible has already been done. Michael is running about like a web-footed idiot, if you'll excuse me saying so; toting up the losses, the damages he'll apply for on tax relief . . . '

Quentin paused. 'He's like a bear with a sore head this morning, especially since his return from the village. He left home practically at the crack of dawn, well before the dam burst.' Then he paused again, eyeing her speculatively and ignoring their small audience being forced to listen to every word. 'Did you see Michael, Jancy?'

'I saw him.'

'So early. It must have been mighty urgent or important.'

She said, lamely: 'He had — things to discuss.'

'I can imagine,' Quentin said, staring hard at her. It was almost as if they were alone, just the two of them in the boutique.

Martin Vigeland cleared his throat noisily and nudged his wife. 'I think, Selma, we had better be getting back to the hotel. We can do no more here, sitting on the stairs. When the water starts receding, then the really hard work will start.'

Leaning against the banister to take the weight off the sprained ankle, Jancy said: 'I'll never be able to thank you people enough.'

Mrs Vigeland shook her head, dismissing the gratitude. 'Please . . . there is no need for thanks. In friendship, in affection, one gives and takes. Who knows when the day will come that you must give in return, to us your kindness and help?'

There was nothing left to say. 'Come along,' Martin Vigeland told his wife, and helped her to her feet.

Sigrid stood up also. 'I might stay a while longer. I'm sure there must be lots of things that I can do.'

A special kind of look passed between her parents. Her father turned to her, trying to restrain a smile. 'No, we find other people who need our hands, people in distress. Is that not right, Mother?'

'It is right,' Selma Vigeland agreed. 'For now we leave and come back later in the day.'

Jancy began to limp down the stairs and the steps covered by the flood-waters. As he noticed the disability Quentin reached for her hand to support her. 'What happened to your foot?'

'She fell,' Sigrid said quickly. 'Down the stairs. A wonder she didn't break a leg.'

'And you kept on working?'

Jancy made a gesture of resignation. 'It's my boutique, my business. I couldn't just sit by and watch other people . . .'

Quentin glanced at Martin. 'This girl — she's so independent . . .'

'They all are,' the older man said with a grin. 'Take my Selma as an example. But would you have them soft and fluttery and useless in a crisis?'

Quentin chuckled. As they all waded through the water to the open doorway, Quentin supported Jancy round the waist.

After final goodbyes, hugs and kisses, the Vigeland family were gone and Jancy turned to re-enter the shop. For a long time she stood there, surveying the deep water lapping at the walls.

Gently Quentin said: 'Listen to me. You're saturated from the waist down practically and you have an injured limb. I'll bet the ankle's black and blue by now. Maybe that's an exaggeration, but, on the other hand, you can't afford to get a bad chill or, worse, pneumonia.'

He went on: 'You've saved the merchandise from water damage and there's not another thing you can do right now except rest up. As Mr Vigeland said, the back-breaking work comes later, the cleaning, the drying-out, the repainting, papering, nailing and glueing timber, weeks and weeks of work.'

She was too tired to care, too tired to argue. Without demuring, she allowed Quentin to accompany her up the stairs and into the bedroom, stacked with cartons and piles of clothing. There was barely room to move about.

'While you're getting out of your wet gear,' he said, 'I'll make some coffee.'

When Quentin returned she had changed into winter pyjamas and was under the bedclothes. He put the steaming coffee mugs on the bedside table and peered through the window.

'Water, water everywhere and not a drop to drink,' he mused. 'It could come to that in a day or two. Meanwhile, don't drink the stuff unless it's boiled.'

Then he sat on the edge of the bed, his blue eyes more vivid than she had ever noticed before, and his unruly hair falling in damp curls over his forehead.

'I think the weather's clearing up,' he said. 'I even saw a patch of blue, enough to make a pair of sailor's trousers.' He smiled. 'You look spent.'

'I feel spent.'

'And your ankle?'

'I'll live.'

'I'm sure you will.' He reached for his hot coffee, staring at her intently over the rim of the stoneware mug. 'Tell me about Michael.'

She was starting to float. Every nerve and muscle in her body was aching and protesting, and she didn't know where she hurt most or hurt least. But she was getting warm under the blankets and her eyes were growing heavy.

'There's nothing to tell.'

'Nonsense,' he retorted gruffly. 'Who do you think you're kidding? You've been kidding me along since our first meeting, outside the hotel. I want to hear about Michael. I have to know, Jancy. Cynthia doesn't want him, I suspect, so there'll be no marriage of convenience there. I hear on the grapevine — Susan's grapevine, that is — that Arnulf Vigeland has asked her to marry him. It's not official yet, but that's a turn-up for the books. That leaves brother Michael out on a limb, high and dry, and that leaves you in an open field. Has he proposed? You're heading for the winning post?'

Jancy closed her eyes and felt the bed rocking. Quentin's voice seemed to be coming from a long distance.

'Yes, he proposed.'

'Did you accept?'

Faintly, she answered: 'I don't love him. I used to think I did. Ever since I came to Bungalan it hasn't been the same. I'm not sure . . . To marry, I'd have to be very sure.'

'Is there someone else, Jancy?'

His firm hand was clasped round her hand, giving her stability as she drifted off. She tried to speak, but the words eluded her.

In her mind, Aunt Edith Talliman was saying: 'If at first you don't succeed, make a pot of tea and try again. Take the plunge and start swimming.'

In all that floodwater? With her sound, sane, old advice, Aunt Edith had been a pillar of strength. Cliches, certainly, but they were as tried and true in her aunt's time as they were today.

Through the cobwebs of approaching sleep she saw the Blue Room she had occupied at the Empire Hotel, and the chintzy room at Irongates. She saw the wall of the boutique being painted in psychedelic colours, the painter perched on his tall ladder, and Cynthia Meddow at the drive-in cinema.

She was in a plane flying to Melbourne, she was in a car driving to

Sydney, and she was in the hotel parlour with Quentin Rickwood.

It was the strangest dream and through it all Aunt Edith Talliman was present, sitting in her favourite chair, or propped up in bed against her numerous pillows, her white-haired serenity casting a curious golden glow on the world of Jancy's subconsciousness.

When she opened her eyes the glow, pale but unmistakably golden, was reflected on the bedspread.

'Hello, Sleeping Beauty,' a voice said, and she saw Quentin at the side of the bed.

'Hello, yourself,' she answered. Her ankle still hurt, but she felt relaxed and refreshed. 'What time is it?'

'Two o'clock.'

Astonished, she said: 'In the afternoon? And I've been lying here all that time?'

'For several hours.'

'And you just sat there, waiting?'

'Someone had to be here.'

The remark touched her deeply. A

strand of hair lay across her face and she brushed it away.

'Is the flooding any worse?'

He gave her an encouraging smile. 'I've been checking regularly. It's going down — fast. Only about a foot of water in the shop now. By tonight it should be all gone.'

She glanced again at the pale glow covering the bed. 'Surely — that can't be sunlight.'

Quentin nodded. 'Pretty feeble, but it's sunlight. The rain has stopped.' And as if to confirm his statement she heard scratchings and scurryings in the guttering outside the bedroom window, followed by the chatter and chirps of bird talk.

'They've come back,' she said, unaccountably pleased. 'The sparrows . . . I haven't heard them, or seen them, in weeks. I rather missed the little busy-bodies . . .'

'I told you,' Quentin reminded her, 'a long time ago. It's the year of the sparrows, with seasons of plenty. Well,' he amended with a chuckle, 'we've had plenty of rain and plenty of floodwater. And plenty of problems . . . '

He reached for her hand and held it tightly, his gaze intense. 'A sparrows' year means money, success, heart's desire and happy endings. You don't have to believe all that, of course — it's only a silly old country saying. But, sometimes, if you want to believe . . . '

Dear Quentin, dear lovable Quentin.

He leaned close to her. 'You're free now, Jancy, arent' you? Quite free.'

She sighed and nodded.

'You can make a fresh start. From scratch.'

'I have to,' she told him.

'I heard,' he said, 'you were contemplating going back to England, selling up in Bungalan, skipping the country and running out on all your friends. Wouldn't you consider staying?'

'For what?' she asked. 'For whom?'

'For me.'

Her eyes widened. 'For you, Quentin?'

'For me,' he repeated firmly.

Her heart skipped a beat and she felt a warm flush mounting her cheeks. Dear Quentin, lovable, loving Quentin. From the beginning he had offered a broad shoulder to lean on, he had helped her establish the business, he had saved her life in the river. Dear, dependable Quentin. Without him there would have been no life.

All those long months when she had been involved with Michael he had remained in the background, trying to protect her and cherishing her from afar. Was that why he had stopped calling and grown morose and difficult?

You fool, she told herself. You blind, stupid little fool. Aunt Edith would be ashamed of you.

'I might — consider staying,' she said.

He leaned further and took her in his arms and kissed her, and she felt the strength and the wanting in him. And the fierce but bridled love of the man.

'What can I do to convince you?' he

asked, stroking her hair.

She raised a hand and laid it tenderly against his smooth-shaven cheek.

'For a start,' she said, 'you could do that again. I've got to get to know you better. And learn to love you.'

'That won't be hard,' he answered. 'But I won't teach you. It will have to grow from within.'

'It's been growing,' she said, 'but I wasn't aware of it. I think it's been there, from that first day, when I saw you leaning against one of the hotel verandah posts.'

Mrs Rickwood, she mused. Mrs Quentin Rickwood. Surely the dragon woman couldn't object to that.

As he kissed her again the sparrows outside set up a shrill chorus of welcome to the emerging sun.

We do hope that you have enjoyed reading this large print book.

Did you know that all of our titles are available for purchase?

We publish a wide range of high quality large print books including:
Romances, Mysteries, Classics
General Fiction
Non Fiction and Westerns

Special interest titles available in large print are:
The Little Oxford Dictionary
Music Book, Song Book
Hymn Book, Service Book

Also available from us courtesy of Oxford University Press:
Young Readers' Dictionary
(large print edition)
Young Readers' Thesaurus
(large print edition)

For further information or a free brochure, please contact us at:
Ulverscroft Large Print Books Ltd.,
The Green, Bradgate Road, Anstey,
Leicester, LE7 7FU, England.
Tel: (00 44) **0116 236 4325**
Fax: (00 44) **0116 234 0205**

Other books in the
Linford Romance Library:

LOVE WILL FIND A WAY

Joan Reeves

Texan Darcy Benton would give anything to be the kind of woman who could captivate her new boss Chase Whitaker. However, the sexy CEO would hardly fall for someone like Darcy, with her straight-laced office wardrobe. Enter Darcy's matchmaking pal, Janet. She transforms her into a bombshell worthy of Chase's undying devotion. Darcy is soon letting her hair down and swapping her boxy suits for slinky dresses. And as Chase becomes intrigued — he's ready for anything . . . including true love.